THE ANNEX

ESSENTIAL TRANSLATIONS SERIES 61

Canada Council for the Arts | Conseil des Arts du Canada

ONTARIO ARTS COUNCIL
CONSEIL DES ARTS DE L'ONTARIO

an Ontario government agency
un organisme du gouvernement de l'Ont

Canada

Guernica Editions Inc. acknowledges the support of
the Canada Council for the Arts and the Ontario Arts Council.
The Ontario Arts Council is an agency of the Government of Ontario.
We acknowledge the financial support of the Government of Canada through the
National Translation Program for Book Publishing, an initiative
of the *Roadmap for Canada's Official Languages 2013-2018:*
Education, Immigration, Communities, for our translation activities.
We acknowledge the financial support of the Government of Canada.
Nous reconnaissons l'appui financier du gouvernement du Canada.

CATHERINE MAVRIKAKIS

THE ANNEX

Translated by Kathryn Gabinet-Kroo

TORONTO—CHICAGO—BUFFALO—LANCASTER (U.K.)

2025

Original title: *L'Annexe*

Guernica Founder: Antonio D'Alfonso

Michael Mirolla, editor
Cover and interior design: Errol F. Richardson

Guernica Editions Inc.
1241 Marble Rock Rd., Gananoque (ON), Canada K7G 2V4
2250 Military Road, Tonawanda, N.Y. 14150-6000 U.S.A.
www.guernicaeditions.com

Distributors:
Independent Publishers Group (IPG)
600 North Pulaski Road, Chicago IL 60624
University of Toronto Press Distribution (UTP)
5201 Dufferin Street, Toronto (ON), Canada M3H 5T8

First edition.
Printed in Canada.

Legal Deposit—Third Quarter
Library of Congress Catalog Card Number: 2025933634
Library and Archives Canada Cataloguing in Publication
Title: The annex / Catherine Mavrikakis ; translated by Kathryn Gabinet-Kroo.
Other titles: Annexe
Names: Mavrikakis, Catherine, 1961- author. | Gabinet-Kroo, Kathryn, 1953- translator.
Series: Essential translations series ; 61.
Description: Series statement: Essential translations series ; 61 | Translation of: L'annexe. | In English, translated from the French.
Identifiers: Canadiana (print) 20250161885 | Canadiana (ebook) 20250165333 | ISBN 9781771839914 (softcover) | ISBN 9781771839921 (EPUB)
Subjects: LCGFT: Novels.
Classification: LCC PS8576.A8579 A6213 2025 | DDC C843/.6—dc23

To the Queen,
if God finds her worth saving.

Chapter 1

This all happened back when I was making yearly pilgrimages to Amsterdam to visit Anne Frank's house. I was travelling around the world when I wasn't looking for an apartment in London. An apartment … She—Anne, that is—had had one for two years. And ever since she left it, people have been visiting the Annex in a steady stream, imagining that after an hour-long wait in line and the proprietor's ten-minute tour, they understood what the Frank family had experienced there. It was back when I couldn't comprehend the notion of having a home, even one in Great Britain. I was camping out in Camden living rooms, squatting the offices of The Broadway in Westminster, and inviting myself into rooms in the Poplar district. I was travelling, too: Turkey, Lebanon, Israel, Libya. I was doing the Middle East. A nomad, that's how I described myself. The vagabond life suited me. My work allowed for it, constantly calling for changes of location and obliging me to stay in hotel rooms in Tel Aviv or Tripoli. And yet, nostalgic for a place I'd never known, I periodically felt the need to settle down. But where? In Tottenham Hale? Why not? I didn't know anyone there, and I didn't care much for the neighbourhood. That was already a good start … Impossible to utter magic words like "There, yes, that's the place, that's definitely the place." Anne Frank hadn't had a choice. One morning, her family had moved across town, leaving the cat behind. They'd had to make it look as if they hadn't really left and that they would very soon be back to feed their pet, or that they'd fled too far to take the little animal with them. They'd convinced themselves that the enemy would see this sacrifice as either proof of the great distance they'd travelled or as a guarantee of their return.

The Franks had moved into the Secret Annex, a miniscule apartment that they'd had to share with the three van Pels—Hermann, Augusta and Peter—and then with Fritz Pfeffer, too. Otto Frank, Anne's father, had arranged everything. As best he could. It was the Annex or deportation … Most of us cannot imagine having less room to manoeuvre. *It couldn't have been easy, all those people crammed together. Stell dir vor, wie überfüllt sie hier waren! Those poor people … a wretched situation, no matter how you look at it! Deve ter estado muito difícil tudo isso* … People looked so serious when they said these things during their visit to "the Anne Frank house." They pictured themselves as fugitive Jews, crowded into a closet-sized space. This story made them go silent for a moment. And then they started up again, losing themselves in trivialities in every language.

Each time I went to the Franks' former apartment, I listened very attentively to the conversations of visitors who were taking a quick, horrified glance at the washroom. They seemed to forget that the eight souls in the Annex had lived not merely with a terrible lack of privacy but with the abject fear of being discovered. The two tiny bits of floor space, hastily hidden by a bookcase, did not simply make up a cramped and uninviting apartment. They served as a hideaway for terrorized occupants who might at any moment be deported. There, the Franks, the van Pels, and Dr. Pfeffer had hoped and had surely lost hope. Then after two years without ever having set foot outside, without ever really even looking outside, with the only light coming from a scrap of sky seen through the attic window, the Annex's tenants had finally gone out for a breath of fresh air on their way to the camps … So one toilet for eight people was not all that traumatic.

It was back when I couldn't fully commit to having a place of my own. I didn't like having a permanent residence, feeling confined for too long in a space that I might make my own. I was happy not having an address. I sprawled out in the impersonal, unadorned rooms of chain hotels. Along the way, I got rid of the things that normal people always end up getting attached to. Everything landed in a garbage can: brushes, clothes, jewellery, books ... I saved no information, I systematically erased all my search histories, I memorized codes, numbers, names, and places. I made sure that I left no trace of myself in the world. I didn't underline in the books that I read, nor did I record even the slightest reference to myself in a notebook or diary. If I liked something, I learned it by heart. Like Fabrice Luchini, I thought with a laugh. Like an actor whose most authentic lines come from rehearsed monologues. I had to avoid creating, even accidentally, a psychological profile. I wore clothes that I didn't particularly like. At airports, I randomly bought crime novels that I didn't hate but that, should they be found in my bag, would reveal nothing about my preferences or my beliefs. I was always on the run. And in my rush forward, I still sometimes wanted a place of my own with a life of my own. But I wasn't holding my breath. My profession did not allow for such expectations. I had chosen it for the sacrifices it required of me, and I did not entertain the hope of one day acquiring a place conducive to a private life. Nevertheless, I ended up back at Anne Frank's apartment every year. The Annex provided me with something; while there, I felt a sense of belonging that had either been lost or had yet to be discovered. A vague urge to have a room of my own, as Woolf wrote, though I had never taken seriously her text on the need to acquire a room in which to write or to live.

Each time I went to Anne Frank's, I stayed a very long time, getting jostled and snapped at by tourists who ultimately did not want to linger in the apartment with the blacked-out windows. I observed them, saw in them their desire to escape. The tour had to be led briskly, *schnell, schnell, vlug, vlug*, make it snappy, so they could quickly reach the screening room located in front of the boutique. There, they could watch a short film about Anne and enjoy the accounts of those who had known and loved her. Some visitors preferred to skip the film and hustled out as fast as they could to buy a poster of Anne Frank and the DVD of the play …

What was I doing, staying so long in the room that Anne Frank had shared for too long with Pfeffer, the dentist? Why did I dawdle in the middle of the room while docile tourists moved in single file against the walls so as not to slow the pace of movement through the rooms set by the audio-guide? Of course, a sign at the entrance to 263 Prinsengracht, the Franks' secret address, invites us to stay as long as we like. Why not stay 25 months as the Franks did?

Squatting the Annex might be a sure way to gain a better understanding of the Franks' existence before they were exterminated. You have to soak up the Annex's atmosphere, its odours, to better experience History, so that the past can present and reveal itself. At least, that's what we're told. But the nudging elbows and exasperated looks of the visitors attached to their audio-guides, not to mention the inhospitable comments made by the guards, who wanted everyone to move fluidly through the Annex, made my prolonged presence at the Franks' fairly incongruous. I had little doubt that Anne and her family would have liked to keep me there with them a little longer. The Frank family and the rest of the household treasured the presence of Miep and Jan and even Bep. Yes, Anne would have invited me to spend the night, close to her. But the others? All these unfriendly pilgrims whom I furtively scrutinized dreamed of seeing me deported like the Franks, whose apartment no one would visit had the family not come to a tragic end.

Every year, twenty million people hurry through the Annex. In the beginning, in 1960, there were fewer people, even though at that time, you could snoop around Anne's place free of charge. But the young lass quickly became a celebrity, thanks to her diary.

Little Annelies's fame saved 263 Prinsengracht from demolition. Someone must have picked up on its commercial potential. Land was very expensive in Amsterdam, and this property was basically an old, dilapidated building like so many others. Proof that the business would be profitable must have been required.

"The Anne Frank House" had undergone several phases of renovations. The original beams and floors had been removed. A passage between the building overlooking the canal and the Annex's upper floor was eventually built. Therefore, modern-day visitors can no longer leave the way they enter, in other words, through the hole created by the moveable bookcase and the narrow stairs that, in 1942, were the only way Anne could access the Annex. These changes, along with the air conditioning, prevent visitors from fully experiencing the confinement of eight human beings in this small space. Especially during the summer … The fresh air makes it impossible to imagine how stifling the atmosphere got up there. But they quickly understand what the inhabitants' state of mind and their living conditions must have been in this place. It really doesn't take that much imagination.

On July 6, 2012, seventy years after Anne and her family had been swallowed up by the Annex, I had just spent more than six hours examining the apartment at 263 Prinsengracht and the indolent tourists who'd come there. I had stayed despite the disparaging comments that I'd endured and that came from visitors who certainly did not want to disrupt the natural rhythm of their Amsterdamian excursion and miss seeing Rembrandt's masterful *Night Watch* at the Rijksmuseum, which closed its doors at 5 p.m. … I knew only too well this passive acceptance of a schedule, the movements of crowds, and the respect for the most asinine rules. This docility deeply disgusted me as it would still do today, were I to stand in line at a museum. Humans comply with the rules; they line up for a ticket, a piece of meat, or death. They would rather submit to these semblances of order than create the slightest hint of chaos in the world. Confusion leads to disaster, as we're so often told; it's instilled in our bones from the moment we start school. The Nazis' strength lay in taking advantage of the species' submissiveness, our innate civility. The Reich's tyranny was founded on the eradication of chaos. Aryans would be Aryans, Jews would be Jews and therefore exterminated, and on that basis, life would seem perfectly clear. The Third Reich was based on a principle of simplicity and order. Everything had to be in its proper place, even people. It was intended as an appeal for a more civilized, more modern way of life …

I go to the Franks' only once a year, and I always stay a little too long, despite the animosity that the other visitors might express for the woman who no longer respects the logic of the line advancing toward the exit … You don't visit friends in a foreign country only to rush off fifteen minutes later. Strangely, I considered the Franks' apartment to be a hospitable place and its former occupants, who were murdered in the camps, to be people who regarded me with kindness.

On that day, July 6, 2012, I had lingered just long enough in Anne's room to begin to feel captive myself. And I had thus come to an absurd conclusion that had few connections to the Franks' life: Having a place of your own is still awful … You end up suffocating in it. No matter what happens, belonging to a place, a scrap of land, or a little apartment is harmful. You end up granting yourself rights, like the right to live. You develop a feeling that is unfounded, a foolish impression regarding the naturality of existence. The place gives this sense of legitimacy to the vanity of human presence in the world. Perhaps that's what Jean-Jacques Rousseau wanted to say at the beginning of his *Discourse on Inequality*: "The first man who, having enclosed a piece of ground, bethought himself of saying *This is mine*, and found people simple enough to believe him, was the real founder of civil society." Culture as we know it begins with the establishment of a place of one's own.

After six hours of voluntary confinement in the Annex, I found myself not far from 263 Prinsengracht, near the canal, and thought about how these sunny streets were surely the last images of Amsterdam that Anne and her family had kept in mind for 25 months. Except for July 6, 1942, it had apparently been raining very hard. "A warm rain fell throughout the day." That's what Anne wrote, and she had no reason to lie. Still, in my line of work, you distrust all witness statements. People never stick to the facts; they see completely insignificant details that they magnify in a subjective way. But in their hiding place, the Franks must have missed these gorgeous canals, and then of course, they also missed the cat. The cat that they'd left behind. But that's another story.

The weather was extremely bad that morning of July 6, 1942, as the Franks entered the Annex, lamenting Holland's soft, drizzly light that so distinguished Vermeer's paintings, which could be admired at the Rijksmuseum if one hurried. The previous day, July 5, a Sunday, Anne's older sister Margot had received a notice summoning her to a German labour camp. The family suspected a ruse. Under no circumstances were German labour camps to be trusted. In Anne's day, the entire world was saying that the internment of populations could only be a hoax. But no more than that. Her mother, upon reception of the letter, sped things along. It wasn't her husband Otto Frank who was being invited to appear before the city authorities but her 16-year-old daughter. They had to leave more quickly than planned. Otto had already prepared almost everything. For months, he had been arranging the family's hideout in a tiny apartment behind his business and a warehouse ... Suddenly, the choice was no longer theirs. So there they are, the four Franks, around 7:30 on the morning of July 6, out on the city streets. Margot bikes off toward the Annex after stuffing her schoolbag full of books. Miep, one of the hideout's guardian angels, has come to get her. Anne walks there with her parents. Her father and mother also carry a satchel and a bag of provisions. It takes a good hour to walk from 37 Merwedeplein to the Annex. I often walked this route, without knowing for sure which streets the Franks had taken. They must have avoided the major boulevards: They didn't want to be noticed.

Anne doesn't know where she's going. Her family has preferred to keep her in the dark. It's only on the way there that bit by bit, her father reveals the plan. Furniture and clothing have already been sent to the place that will serve as their hideaway ... the summons has simply hurried things along. The hideaway is on Prinsengracht. It won't be anything like a house. Anne learns of the family's survival plan as she walks; she is terribly hot. On that July 6, Annelies Frank is wearing numerous layers of clothing so that they don't have to drag heavy luggage across Amsterdam, attracting attention. No Jew in their situation would have risked leaving home with a suitcase full of clothes. Anne has put on "two undershirts, three pairs of underpants, a dress, and over that a skirt, a jacket, a raincoat, two pairs of stockings, heavy shoes, a cap, a scarf, and lots more ..." Later, she'll make note of it in her diary.

Along the way, people stare at them. These are labourers going to work, very early. They seem to feel sorry for the morning's pedestrians. They have understood. The yellow star sewn onto the family's clothes cannot help but indicate the reason for such occurrences. But they prefer to forget. That's how I picture it. Despite their eyes full of pity, they offer no vehicle nor the least bit of assistance to the family wandering through Amsterdam on this early summer day.

On the way, Anne is thinking of the cat they left behind, at home. Is it the cat that creates a feeling of belonging?

The Franks had fled Frankfurt. Hitler's arrival in 1933 had turned Jews like them into stateless individuals. The parents tried to "make a new life," as they say, to acquire a country of their own, in Amsterdam. At the time, this strategy seemed to be a fairly good idea, and besides, Amsterdam was known for its hospitality. Historically, the city had often presented itself as a land of refuge. In the 16th century, William the Silent had turned the United Provinces into a region of religious tolerance. Many were those who found it a safe place to practice their faith and lead a peaceful life—Jews from the Iberian Peninsula, Protestants, and Huguenots. Amsterdam … it must have represented hope for those who no longer had a place of their own. Edith and Otto Frank, who were educated people, had surely thought that this city could protect them. After all, it had helped others in their time of need. And Edith's maiden name was Hollander. This name must have played a role in the decision, acting as a sign. They would not be in any danger in Holland. They couldn't have imagined that in 1940, the country would be invaded by the German army despite all the good omens.

Life and my profession taught me well … I learned never to trust omens, never to cherish any hope, never to read people to find a clue, a signal, or a gesture in my favour. Life couldn't care less about me. And it has nothing to tell me.

I was thinking about all kinds of things as I left the Annex and lit a cigarette on the sidewalk not very far from Prinsengracht. I was thinking that someone at work could confirm the accuracy of what Anne Frank had written about the rain in Amsterdam on July 6, 1942. According to the young girl, on Sunday the 5th, the day Margot received the summons, Amsterdam had been oppressively hot. Had she told the truth? I was also wondering what had happened to the Frank family's cat. I seemed to remember reading that the neighbours had welcomed the cat into their home. The Franks had left the cat a pound of meat to sustain it through the first days of their absence. And then afterwards, the neighbours had let it stay in their apartment. A different tomcat ruled over the Annex, chasing rats away from the stores of food. There was also Peter van Pels' cat, which he'd been able to bring into hiding with him. But Anne Frank's cat had been abandoned and that I had trouble getting over. Just as Anne had. And while I smoked, I thought about the fact that nowadays, you aren't even allowed to bring your dog to Anne's house. And that animals are forbidden in what is now called the Anne Frank Museum, and that I found this restriction very sad, without really knowing why. Anne herself had pined for her cat for a long time. Like me, Anne would have been shocked to know that after her death, animals were barred from the Annex whereas the rules for communal life conceived by Mr. van Pels had included special care for small domestic animals. Times have changed ... and not so much for the better.

I had just finished my Lucky. I was lost in thoughts about the name of Anne's cat, which I couldn't remember, and about Amsterdam's climate in the 1940s, when instinct brutally yanked me back from the hazy past in which I was losing myself ... I was being followed. Not too far off, a big dark-haired man was trying not to look at me. He actually turned his back to me. I'd seen him earlier at the Franks'. He had appeared to be waiting for me in Anne's room. Then, afraid of being spotted, had quickly fled.

This was not the first time since my arrival in the Netherlands, legendary home away from home, that I noticed someone dogging my footsteps. In my line of work, being tailed is something quite common, alarming as it may be. This guy had to be working for Echthros, as we called the enemy organization. I knew that my last assignment had brought some trouble my way, even though I'd been hastily extracted. I'd come out of it somewhat the worse for wear.

Automatically, I began to feel for my pistol, a Glock 9 mm semi-automatic that I kept in the bottom of my bag. I definitely had it with me at Anne's. I lived like this, never knowing when I might have to kill someone. I wish the Franks had had a pistol as nice as mine and had been trained to kill … A weapon would have kept them from dying in the camps. Anne might have been killed as soon as she was arrested, but one can always hope. Foolishly, we hesitate before taking our own life or someone else's. In my case, for my job, I had learned not to hem and haw … Quick action had been a major part of my training. I thus envisioned taking down the big dark-haired guy whom I had just realized was stalking me. First, I had to rapidly assess the risks and make a quick decision. This man could also be a nutcase who was foolishly mistaking me for an artist. He might be thinking that I had made a performance piece of staying in Anne Frank's room for such an extended period. I wouldn't have been the first to squat Anne Frank's house in the name of art. Who's to know?

I didn't think. Accustomed to various methods of surveillance and escape, I instinctively headed for the tour boats, the "Hop-On-Hop-Offs" that take you around the city, stopping from time to time at the biggest tourist attractions. I knew that using my gun in the middle of Amsterdam was not the best plan. A better idea was to stick with making a run for it. My training at Agathos had taught me that. At least I could enjoy myself while I learned the history of the city's canals.

I had no desire to return to my here-and-now when I'd found it so peaceful to wander through the 1940s with Anne and her family. I would have stayed longer, relaxing at home in the Annex, in an almost familiar past. But a boat seemed ready to get underway.

I briskly headed over to the sales counter that I had spotted just across from the dock and bought myself a ticket. The shady character tried to do the same, but there was no more room for him. All the seats had been sold. From the corner of my eye, I could see him arguing in vain with the employee at the counter. You're out of luck, my friend, I thought with a smile ... I quickly understood that he had no interest in gunning someone down in public either. Not in the middle of Amsterdam, not right in front of the tour boats. It would be too hard for him to make his escape after killing me. Amsterdam is not exactly the best place for executing spies in broad daylight ... The guy would probably wait for me in my hotel room instead.

I boarded the boat, which was actually very crowded, easily if not too easily rid—so I thought—of that man who surely did not wish me well and who must finally have recognized something other than the artist in me.

I sat in the last remaining seat, next to two young Japanese women dressed in Gothic style and looking as pale as Anne Frank must have looked to her unfamiliar neighbours when she left the Annex to go to her death after spending two years inside those darkened rooms. In any case, my cruise through the canals of Amsterdam went smoothly. I savoured the pleasures that had been denied the Franks for 25 months, while the sumptuous city spread out just around the corner from their pitiful hideaway. Behind me, a father spoke Russian, threatening to take his unruly sons back to Anne Frank's house and leave them there, inside, if they kept on yelling in the boat. This conversation did not seem to have much of an effect on the boys, who were shouting as they horsed around. It was 2012 ... The thought of being confined in Anne Frank's house no longer scared children, who had surely developed different fears since the end of the Second World War.

The boat was about to dock in front of the Rijksmuseum when I received a message from work on my cell phone. It bore a code number that I knew only too well and had, in fact, been dreading for some time … It meant that I was to go directly to the airport and catch the first available flight. From whichever city I landed in, I was to take another flight to Tel Aviv. Someone would meet me there. I got off the tour boat in front of Central Station West, making sure that I was not still being followed. Momentarily reassured, I hailed a taxi after having waited several minutes before seeing one pass by. Inside the car, I kept a firm grip on my weapon. I asked the driver to take me straight to Schiphol Airport, where I boarded the first airplane that was taking off. I didn't even stop at the hotel to collect my personal effects. The guy must have gone there, unless he'd thought to go straight to the airport. But he apparently hadn't realized that I'd spotted him, and I left Amsterdam without incident.

As fate would have it, I ended up in Reykjavik, where strangely I had never been despite all the travelling I'd done for my job, but I saw nothing of Iceland and its fabled volcanoes. Agathos had sent new encrypted instructions to my telephone. Tel Aviv was a no-go. New York was my new destination, so I boarded a Boeing heading there instead. I obeyed orders. Without even thinking about it. The situation seemed serious, and the man who'd spotted me at Anne's had been tasked with killing me.

So I had regretfully left Amsterdam, the city of Anne Frank, behind me. Before leaving the city, I would have liked to return to the Annex once or twice to spend some more time there. I would have revisited the big warehouse and tried to detect the scents of cinnamon, clove, and pepper, which were prepared in the mill room back in the day. I would have tried to picture Anne and her sister washing in an improvised bathroom that they created in the office every Sunday. I would have felt Anne's fear when she and her family went down to the warehouse to listen to Radio London, and I would have trembled in terror with her at the thought that they might be overheard. My swift getaway had just deprived me of these moments with Anne, and I was very angry at the guy for having found me in Amsterdam rather than in Paris or even London, where I lived for a few months of the year. In a certain sense, he had just torn me away from my family.

In the plane taking me to the United States, I couldn't stop thinking about the occupants of 263 Prinsengracht and their life during all those months of seclusion. Two years seemed like an eternity to me. They'd had to adapt to a state of constant vigilance.

I unzipped my black messenger bag. I'd dumped my Glock in a trash can in Amsterdam. I felt a bit naked, even though I knew I'd be getting another weapon when I reached my destination. Inside the bag was a copy of the *Diary of Anne Frank*, which I had just purchased at the Annex shop. I also had three postcards with Anne's lovely face smiling at me. I opened the diary at random. On page 44, I read these sentences, which seemed quite appropriate: "… I've asked myself again and again whether it wouldn't have been better if we hadn't gone into hiding, if we were dead now and didn't have to go through this misery, especially so that the others could be spared the burden. But we all shrink from the thought. We still love life, we haven't forgotten the voice of nature, and we keep hoping, hoping for … everything."

When we landed in New York, I did not get off with the other passengers. A text message told me to sit tight until my chaperones arrived. All of the plane's occupants left the aircraft happy to be done with the somewhat cramped cabin that they'd occupied for eight hours and in which they'd begun to feel a little confined. They clearly lacked Anne Frank's fortitude.

After a moment, two female American Secret Service agents came to find me in the plane's cabin. I couldn't leave the 747 unless flanked by these two guard dogs. They implied that a safe house had been found for me. We had to hurry there. I was in danger of being kidnapped, tortured, or simply killed in the street.

That is what I understood, even though the two women protecting me were not particularly talkative.

Without ever entering the airport itself, they escorted me to an ordinary-looking minivan in which I was driven along a runway. We had to take a small plane that would fly me to a city whose name I was not to know. I would be blindfolded until we landed. But due to an indiscretion on the part of one of my guards, who casually mentioned to the other that she was going to Schwartz's to eat a smoked-meat sandwich as soon as she completed my transfer, I immediately knew that we were heading to Montreal and that I just might be able to escape my fate.

Chapter 2

I didn't know Montreal well. I had, however, been there twice as a child. My mother had spent her youth there in the 1950s, and she'd decided that, during the long Easter holidays accorded by Swiss schools, I should stay with her at the home of my grandparents, who were both already in their 80s. So I was there in March 1975 and April 1976, as the season hesitated to give way to springtime. We had celebrated the new year together, at my mother's place, in Nice. On January 2, I'd gone back to my boarding school in the heart of the Alps, and in early February, I'd received a plane ticket to Montreal along with a little purple card with "See you soon, darling, from your Mama who loves you" penned in red, which had briefly given me back a sense of belonging.

I remember marvellous moments in the airplane when, bursting with hope, I'd felt like I was flying off to paradise, melancholy arrivals at Mirabel after hours over the Atlantic, and especially the interminable time spent at the airport. As I recall, my mother's flight had been delayed both times I travelled to meet her. Her plane had landed a few hours after mine, late in the day, and I'd had to wait there, sitting on a chair under the stewardess's kind and watchful eye, hoping that my mother would come get me.

Mama had appeared bright-eyed and bushy-tailed after a full day of travel, in a hurry, and happy to see me even as she chastised me for being slow. We had taxied downtown together, making up for the time we'd lost. I had told her about my friends, my teachers, my academic standing, my literary aspirations, and my foreign language awards. She had told me about the beginning of her year, her travels, and her very sweet life with her new girlfriend Virginia, an extravagant and generous woman whom I actually liked a lot. I had grown taller and thinner, and I was still dressed like a frump, a real tomboy, my worried mother remarked. She had bought me beautiful clothes in Paris. She was trying to put on a good show in front of Grandpa and Grandma, who didn't notice such details and whom she was, nevertheless, trying to impress.

I loved Mama a lot; she was beautiful, blond, and funny, even though I did not in fact know her very well. I could have listed a few of her principal character traits such as her good taste, her vivaciousness, her flirtatiousness, her irony, and her resilience. However, I would not have been able to add much more to this too brief list to successfully paint an interesting or comprehensive portrait of her. Since the age of five, I'd spent almost 10 months a year at the Berg Boarding School in the Swiss mountains, not far from Lausanne. During the summer, I could be found at a camp for children or teens in Israel. When I was very young, I'd lived in Paris with Mama and Alexandra, her ex-girlfriend, but our life together had made little impression on me. That which others call childhood, with the nostalgia and emotion that this word can entail, had unfolded for me in Montreal, the two times I visited Grandpa and Grandma during Easter vacation.

At the time, my grandparents occupied a large dwelling on Saint-Urbain, not far from the École des Beaux-Arts, in the heart of downtown Montreal. They rented it—I remember the expression my mother used—"for peanuts." My grandfather had been an unknown painter. My grandmother had supported the household by teaching dance, after having been employed as a ballerina in a corps de ballet. My mother had inherited her own mother's passion for dance, and whenever she'd had the chance, she'd taken me to see performances at the Opera.

My grandparents led a very modest, bohemian existence, of which Mama was somewhat ashamed. At least, that's what I'd gathered. My two visits with Grandpa and Grandma had seemed like holidays, even though we hadn't celebrated the Christian Easter. My grandparents had succeeded in turning our presence in their home into an unforgettable experience.

Mama and I hadn't gone out much in Montreal, except to attend dinners that my mother's relatives had given in our honour. Everyone had showered me with gifts. To me, Montreal seemed like a very nice place. And I'd often heard talk of the city itself because my mother spoke so enthusiastically about the places where she'd spent her own childhood. "Schwartz's" was one of the words that cast Mama back to a bygone, mythical era. There were other words: Warshaw, Mount Royal, Morgan's, Saint-Lawrence Boulevard, and of course, Beaver Lake. Uttering one of these magical terms was all it took to make her happy, and at the end of her life, I took advantage of this little fact about her to make her smile.

At the American Hospital of Paris, in Neuilly, when she was dying of breast cancer and suffering terribly, Mama had asked that I be the one to look after her. She'd had me called to her bedside, and despite our somewhat distant relationship, she had asked me to accompany her on this strange voyage toward death. This decision may seem fairly surprising. Mama was very young when she'd had four daughters to whom she might have felt closer than she did to me, the result of a marriage prior to her brief encounter with my father. She had raised these girls, the Americans. They had grown up with her, and Mama had tried to mold their character. But when it came to asking someone to escort her to her death, she thought of me, her Swiss daughter, as precise as clockwork, her foreigner, her tomboy. I had the temperament for this sort of thing, she said. She considered my sisters, although much older, to be faint of heart, like their father. My own progenitor had behaved like an imbecile but, according to my mother, he'd never been afraid of anything. I had inherited his composure, his sense of duty, his work ethic, and his sense of urgency, and Mama had long feared that I would enlist in the army as my father had decided to do when he was very young. In fact, he had become a career officer. My mother tried to protect me from this spell that she herself had cast when she reminded me that Simon, my father, had died in the Six Day War, before I was even born. According to my mother, the army was in no way, shape, or form a wise choice. She was afraid that I was too much the daughter of the one she affectionately and jokingly called "our dearly departed."

During the final months of Mama's life, I spent all my time at her side in the big blue leatherette armchair to the right of her hospital bed—her death bed—or on a mattress that had been laid next to her. Strangely, I had developed pneumonia and had ended up being treated in the same place as my mother, so that I wouldn't have to leave her. One of her doctors who came to speak to her had insisted that I immediately get tested. My breathing had troubled her. I was sick. I had to get well.

I was a literature student back then and so had immediately imagined she was in the Thomas Bernhard novel in which the grandson and the grandfather are hospitalized at the same time, and despite my anguish, I'd found some consolation in this literary echo. Anyway, Mama and I had never slept together in our entire life. I had always hoped to spend the night with my mother. Her illness became a blessed time when I could finally dream as I lay next to her and ask her when she awoke how she was feeling.

I was as faithful to my post as a soldier, she used to tell the people who came to visit her. Her companion Virginia had insisted numerous times that Mama should be brought back to the house to be cared for by a number of nurses. That way, she could spend her final weeks of life at home, in Nice. But Mama wanted to die in a place less familiar than the one that money could provide for her. She'd lived like a queen for over 40 years. She maintained that she wanted to die the way ordinary people do. At least that was what she said. With death so near, she couldn't afford to be capricious. She knew very well that the end-of-life journey was harsh. And she also thought that dying at home would be even more difficult than dying in the hospital. How could she agree to leave such comfort and the beauty she was used to having around her? Arranging for her somewhat shoddy care was already a bereavement. The forswearing of a life of ease was an inevitable step toward the death that Mama wanted to experience. She was in too much pain.

I knew that my mother was from an era when people still remembered that close European relatives had perished under horrific conditions in camps or during the war. Thus there was no reason to complain about dying at 62 in a fancy hospital in a Paris suburb.

Despite the troubling doses of morphine, Mama still managed to smile when I asked her to tell me about her outings with her girlfriends to Kresge, which had opened a big store on Sainte-Catherine Street in 1953. That's where the girls bought their nail polish, stockings, and lipstick.

In fact, as she lay dying, Mama spoke only of Montreal, the city where she'd been so happy with her parents, cousins, and friends. She'd left that life for good in 1947 to go live with her first husband in London, then briefly in Moscow. It was during a trip to Greece in the 1960s that she'd been seduced by my father, with whom she'd lived for less than a year … After Papa's death, she'd wandered across Europe with the infant me, and had then met Alexandra at a cousin's home in Paris. She had ended up settling in France, a country that she regarded as mythical, then moved to the south, to Nice. But she clearly felt great nostalgia, tinged with disdain, for her slightly eccentric life with Grandpa and Grandma, and for Montreal, her marvellous *chez-soi*, her *heym*.

In recent years, I had avoided thinking about safe houses, which are however, sooner or later, the fate of people like me, just as I had avoided the thought of my assassination in an ultramodern hotel room or in front of Anne Frank's lovely house. I took one day at a time. Finding myself back in Canada, in Quebec no less, practically back home with my grandmother and grandfather (who had both been dead for a very long time), filled me with joy, even though under the conditions of protective custody for which I was already preparing, I would not be able to enjoy the area. I wouldn't be going out very often … Presumably, I would be under house arrest indefinitely, and I wouldn't be free to walk in the parks or stroll along the tranquil Montreal streets whose names I was trying in vain to remember. I had messed up my exfiltration. It was in my best interest to disappear quickly. I was going underground; it stood to reason. I would be swallowed up by this giant black hole, my absence from the world. I wasn't convinced that I'd make it out of this adventure alive and, in reality, my end mattered little to me. I'd known a certain number of agents who'd disappeared without leaving the least trace. Perhaps they were dead or, when they'd left their refuge, had had to further erase whatever trace was left of their identity. So there it was, the life and death I'd chosen for myself. I couldn't complain.

During the trip from the airport to the lodgings that would be my home, I did not regret the freedom that was being taken from me for an unspecified period of time. Instead, I felt a real and rare sense of happiness: I, who had learned never to see events in my favour, shouldn't I read this wonderful coincidence as a sign of something? While I'd never had any real homeland, other than the one that my job assigned me, I was winding up in a hospitable city that my mother had once loved. From beyond the grave, my family was opening its arms to me.

Arriving at our destination blindfolded and unable to determine exactly where I was, I was able to inhale 45 seconds worth of Montreal's humid July air. The day had begun the previous night in Europe, in the Franks' apartment; it was ending on a summer evening in North America, perhaps not too far from my grandparents' former apartment.

I clung to the idea of Montreal. I was sure I'd correctly interpreted the words of the guard guiding me with a firm grasp on my arm. She definitely relished the idea of a well-earned smoked-meat. At Schwartz's, yes, at Schwartz's.

Mama had told me a lot about the Montreal summer's mugginess, capable of triggering violent thunderstorms. Sometimes in Nice, she congratulated herself for having left Quebec's climate to live under more clement skies. My grandparents had always teased their daughter about her aversion to Montreal's extreme cold and heat. They predicted that, despite all her efforts, she would one day be obliged to return to Quebec to pay a visit to her Swiss Miss (that was their nickname for me), who would've returned to live in their country. Were my grandparents ever wrong! Mama died when I was very young. Perhaps following her wishes, I had not chosen North America to be my continent. And now according to all appearances, incongruously, I was returning home to the unbearable humidity of summer in the city to meet my death, or something of the sort, in Montreal.

I knew nothing about July or August in Quebec, but the climate, or whatever I could quickly make of it as we got out of the minivan, seemed familiar to me. The air was already heavy, much clammier than it had been in Amsterdam during the past few days, and my overly warm clothes stuck to my skin as we rushed into what I understood to be a building. We crossed a space that must have been the basement and the garages of a vast edifice. It would house, I was only too sure, my own personal Annex.

Anne Frank, whose diary I'd reread for the umpteenth time while crossing the Atlantic, came to mind. Her words kept me company. The first night in the hideout had not been very easy for either Anne or her family. She wrote that she had instantly understood that she could never feel at home in the Annex. At the beginning of her confinement, she'd had the curious impression that she was sort of vacationing at a rather bizarre boarding-house. Since I'd never had a home of my own, there was little chance I'd feel nostalgic for some place in my past. Everything would be easy.

We took an elevator. The metal door was extremely old. I thought I recognized the sound of an ancient mechanism, like an accordion, which I immediately associated with a memory from Europe. I couldn't imagine finding in the modern city that I assumed to be Montreal, such outdated devices, leading me to conclude that my patrons had found an old rattrap in one of the city's sordid neighbourhoods in which to slowly kill off agents who, like me, had become too troublesome.

My footsteps and those of the two American women guarding me reverberated on the lobby floor. We took care not to create a racket with our three bodies. It was very late. The vibrations of an intense musical rhythm reached us from a distant apartment. It was a Saturday night, and some young people must have organized a big party. For reasons of security, my two guard dogs were adamant that we meet no one on the way to our final destination. They asked me to take off my wooden sandals, which were clacking on the floor. The guard maintaining her grip on my right arm helped me. Her movements seemed powerful. The strength of her hands reassured me.

Since the beginning of my trip in the company of these women, I'd thought that I was dealing with two dimwits, two matrons who mindlessly carried out orders. But the one firmly holding my arm managed, perhaps in spite of herself, to demonstrate a certain benevolence through her precise movements. I was going to arrive safe and sound. I could breathe a little. I had spent 36 hours functioning on constant alert with the possibility of being gunned down before reaching my destination. I was alone in the world, without a single possession. I had left my personal effects at the Amsterdam Hilton. At the very least, I deserved my own bed.

After going down a long corridor, we stopped in front of an apartment, whose door the other guard hurriedly opened. Only after having closed the heavy door behind me and double locking it did the two women guide me by the shoulders through a series of rooms that seemed to me like a maze. They finally sat me on a bed. With my eyes blindfolded, I couldn't see their faces. However, I recalled that when they'd collected me on the plane in New York, I had taken a good long look at them. I thought at the time that they looked like me. Their faces were like mine after years in the secret service. They no longer had their own features, no longer had a real expression. They no longer inhabited their bodies. They had, in a way, abandoned them, hoping to find that they were somewhere other than where they were. That's what I thought about myself when from time to time, I caught a glimpse of my silhouette in a hotel room mirror. I'd lost the ability to produce a slightly odd duplicate of myself, to leave a trace of my existence, or even to feel my shadow's existence.

My two guards indicated that I had to stay there, alone. It was getting late; they were leaving. The next day, a certain Otto would come deal with me. He wasn't on duty that night. I had only to go to sleep. One of the women kindly wished me good luck. Chuckling, I told her to toast to my good health as she dined on her smoked-meat sandwich! Schwartz's might still be open, and if not, across the street, The Main Deli was open 24 hours a day, if things hadn't changed since my adolescence years ago. The only response I got was the sound of a key rattling in the lock and the footsteps of the two guards echoing in the hallway. They were angry that they'd let on where I was. At least that's how I interpreted their hurried escape. In their haste, they'd even forgotten to remove the blindfold they'd put over my eyes at the airport. I found myself thus unable to see and locked up in a room somewhere in a Montreal neighbourhood that I would have loved to explore.

Sitting on the edge of what would henceforth be my bed, I reviewed the mental images of the past two days' rush of events. Everything had happened too fast. Tailing me were Echthros agents determined to kill me wherever in the world I might be found. The people handling my case could have found a way to put a bullet in my head in the middle of the Reykjavik airport or aboard the plane. And if they'd failed to do so, it was merely a matter of luck. I had truly "dodged a bullet." I'd just avoided death or even torture. I'd killed a couple of rival spies from whom I'd obtained precious information about the enemy Organization. Nothing had happened to me since I'd been shadowed by the guy I'd noticed in front of Anne's house, 36 hours earlier. I had arrived safely in Montreal. This story had a happy ending. For the time being. I would be able to regain my strength. I'd worry about the future later.

And there, seated on the edge of the bed that I dared not leave, I finally felt safe. In the dark, with my eyes blindfolded, I was gripped by a paralysis that seemed certain to delay the crazy progression of events and postpone the moment of my death.

I could still hear the faint echoing of the guards' receding steps and of the sounds of closing doors, then nothing more. The party music that I'd heard as we walked through the building's corridors no longer reached me. There was total silence. It didn't seem threatening.

Inside the room, an intense, benevolent warmth enveloped me. Very slowly, I managed to remove the blindfold. The darkness surrounding me was thick. Heavy curtains prevented outside light from entering. Just one tiny ray poorly defined a few contours. I could make out the shapes of a nightstand to my right and a big dresser facing the bed. The sheets I was sitting on gave off a pale glow. I suddenly felt how terribly exhausted I was by the trip I'd just made. I wasn't even tempted to turn on the light that I could just make out on the nightstand next to the bed. The darkness was mine. It would soon lead me toward sleep, soothing me. I felt my way around the bed, brushed by the dresser, and discovered a big piece of furniture with many shelves filled with books. I left the exploration of this promising little library for the next day. I would have plenty of time to consult the works placed there … After all, reading had once been my life … I went toward the window. I pulled the curtains back a bit to look outside.

My room opened onto an interior courtyard flanked by three buildings' walls. A distant streetlight weakly lit the enclave. Apparently, moss grew in this humid place. And I assumed that the sun must rarely shine in this foul swamp, even at midday. I was on the first floor. Far away, diagonally across from my window, behind a high hedge, the few parked cars that I could barely see proved the presence of human life. Before me rose monotonous banks of windows, and yet they allowed no light to escape. Probably very few people lived in this building where I was going to be hiding, or else thick curtains, like those I'd just parted, prevented the occupants from revealing their existence to others. Where on earth could the party whose joyful sounds I'd heard have been held? Above the courtyard, I saw a bit of low sky. The sky over Montreal, my family's Montreal. There is always sky in this world. Even Anne Frank contemplated the azure from deep within her Annex. At least that's what I liked to believe.

A bolt of lightning split the sky. A deafening noise followed. The thunder was violent. Rain struck the pane through which I was observing the courtyard. I wanted to enjoy the air that the wind and the water were bringing me. I raised the sash window without a hitch and realized that I wasn't as imprisoned as the two guards had led me to believe when they locked the door behind them. I could flee through the window, crossing the little yard created by the building. A fire escape was waiting to lead me, if I so wished, down from my first floor to terra firma. For a few seconds, I was tempted to run away, leave my refuge, and refuse the protection offered by the services of Agathos, my employer. I was still free to choose my destiny. But I knew immediately that this would be a mistake. For fun, rather than out of conviction, I made a very short list of people in Montreal who could help me, but in fact I no longer knew anyone in the city. The members of my big maternal family bore the name that I'd had up until my entry into the secret service, and I thought that I might be able to find someone who would treat me kindly for a few days. However, after a while, my relatives' homes would be the first place that agents from my country or from enemy countries would go to scoop me up. My employer had known everything about me for quite some time. For over 20 years, the organization had managed to appropriate all traces of my past. I had nothing left. A few vague memories that it had been wise to relinquish. No, it was best to do the smart thing. I would stay in my room, which seemed hospitable enough. This so-called Otto would come the next day to organize my life, and then I'd see. Perhaps one day, I'd sneak out and put my feet on the courtyard's iron rungs. But for the moment, I only had to wash up in the bathroom that I'd just noticed at the opposite end of my room.

After taking a shower in the dark and drinking water straight from the faucet, I decided to go to bed. It felt unexpectedly good, and I stretched out my full length on the sheets, with a hand towel wrapped just around my hips. My cheek bumped up against something. Three well-wrapped squares of chocolate invited me to indulge my taste buds, to feel comforted. They were like the little pieces of chocolate that you find on the beds in luxury hotels. Who had been so considerate as to leave sweets there for me? The chocolate was good, and I swallowed the three morsels with great satisfaction. Buried in my bag were the two or three Toblerone bars I'd put there after picking them up at Schiphol for the trip. Chocolate had always been the guilty pleasure of the person I'd learned to be. It was a fictional preference that I'd adopted in the beginning, to create an identity that was not my own. When I was young, in Switzerland, I'd been known as the quirky girl who didn't like chocolate. I'd learned to like it for my job. I'd also decided to become a smoker. I had thus manipulated quite a few aspects of my personality in order to cease being myself. One day, a co-worker had laughingly predicted that chocolate would give me away, that enemies would locate me by following my trail of candy wrappers. Back then, I'd laughed, not wanting to explain to her that chocolate really wasn't my thing, but now I realized how right she may have been. I'd just pounced on the chocolate squares when I could simply have had myself a little smoke.

Lying on the sheets in my new room that night, I again thought of Anne Frank. Little Anne has not fully described what she felt that first night in the Annex. She prefers to stick to the facts, to write about how she settled in. She and her father put away the crates, unpack the boxes, fill the closets, make the beds. Her mother and sister are too stunned by what is happening to them to rouse themselves. Anne, like her father, prefers to move. She doesn't think; she takes action. The first night, she was surely exhausted by the day she'd had. This exhaustion is not recorded in Anne Frank's diary, but one can imagine. I myself had nothing to put away, no familiar object that welcomed me and whose placement I could choose. Unlike Anne Frank, I had no apartment of my own to lament and that I'd had to abandon. I had no cat to cry over, not even a real lover, a Peter to miss. I had no one

… My parents had long been dead. I'd executed a couple who had trusted me and whom I'd befriended for two relatively happy years. I had chosen an occupation for which you must very quickly erase all traces of yourself, one that does not permit any form of attachment. I had opted for a sort of religious vocation, but it didn't even seem that sad. I regretted nothing.

I sprawled out in the freshness that the storm and my shower had provided. This new bed with its clean, very white sheets felt like it was mine. Presumably someone had made it for me. I'd never really had my own bed. Except in Montreal, at my grandparents' place, where Grandma had arranged a little room for me during my two visits, and maybe also in Mama's hospital room, if I counted the mattress or armchair that I'd slept on at the time. Anne Frank herself believed from the moment she arrived that she'd never feel at home in the Annex, but I suspected that I could build myself a future in the room I'd just discovered.

I heard a far-off cry that split the night. I sat bolt upright; I must have nodded off a bit. Apparently the stridency of the sound had awakened me. But it was nothing. The doleful clamor of the city as it heated up in the night. But by force of habit, I started looking for the pistol that I'd tossed into a garbage can some 36 hours ago earlier at Schiphol, having been very careful not to let anyone see me. Pointless, then, to scrounge around in the bag that my two guards had left at the foot of my bed. Again out of habit, I turned to open the nightstand. The secret service would never have left me without a weapon. You were always expected to defend yourself or to kill yourself before being captured by the enemy. Indeed, a 9 mm Sig Sauer P228 Parabellum with a box of bullets was waiting for me in the drawer. Without thinking, I loaded it. Then I put it next to me, on my bed.

I fell blissfully asleep. Like Hans Castorp at the Sanatorium Berghof, I felt that I'd finally come home.

Chapter 3

The door of my room banged open with complete disregard for the gentle sleep in which I was immersed. I woke up abruptly. I reflexively grabbed the Sig Sauer that was beside me as I slept. I immediately took aim at the intruder entering my room unannounced. I had just enough time to pull last night's towel over my bare body and already I was prepared to defend myself. Despite the room's prevailing obscurity, I could make out a large man, his arms laden with a heavy tray piled high with croissants and chocolate Danishes. The hot pastry mixed with melted chocolate emitted an intoxicating aroma. I was very hungry, as I quickly realized. For hours, I'd had nothing to eat but three little bites of chocolate. But even tormented by the mad desire to fill my belly, I held onto my gun and waited to learn what was happening to me.

I'd been dreaming that I was in the middle of a meal, but my reverie was cruelly interrupted with a shuddering of my body. And too, someone had played with the lock on a door, compelling me to jump up and shake myself awake. A man was entering my sanctuary with a delicious-looking breakfast. Should I be suspicious or not? Was I to shoot him down immediately, before he drew a weapon? Were his laden arms really a sign of his good will and his defenselessness? My gun was still protecting me. I was going to have to make a decision.

"But you're absolutely mad, Bella, to greet me like that," the man said lightly, giving the impression of being unconcerned about the weapon I was pointing at him. "I brought you some sustenance. It's your first day with us, here at the Budapest Hotel. Excuse me, the Grand Budapest Hotel … Welcome home. I must celebrate the arrivals of my guests … You've seen the film, right? You know, the Wes Anderson movie … It's terribly funny. Nothing to do with the Bates Motel, if you know what I mean. Yes, Alfred Hitchcock's motel … I hope you won't feel like that here … I wasn't able to come greet you last night. I'm so sorry about that, my dear! I won't do it again. But with everything I have to think about … The arrivals and departures … I don't stop! Six of you arrived last night. You didn't hear anything, did you? I gave you the best room, the one at the back … But then you must sleep like a baby, right? You've come from far away, haven't you? No need to answer. In any case, I'd advise you, my dear, not to reveal anything at all about your past. Make something up … You *are* in a movie or a novel, after all … It will actually seem rather like *Grand Hotel* here. This kind of place leads us into intrigues, whether we like it or not. Greta Garbo and Joan Crawford, they're splendid in it … And Lionel Barrymore! *Maravilloso*! A treasure. Do you see yourself more as Joan or as Greta? I have a hard time imagining you fully clothed, but at first glance, I see you as being more like the Divine. 'I want to be alone.' That's *her* line in *Grand Hotel* … She says those words with disdain … 'I want to be alone' … Brilliant … I'll bring you the movie, you can see for yourself. But you remind me of Garbo before she starts to speak … Yes, you're in the silent movie, and you keep staring at me with your big moony eyes … Yes, you must see Garbo when she begins to have a voice, you'll find her inspiring … I won't forget about the video. You'll see that we're equipped here, and you can order anything you like from me. You're not in some cheap hotel here or in a Texas prison, dearest … You'll be treated like a queen. Ask and ye shall receive. Isn't that what Christ would say? Things are arranged so that you'll forget where you live … This has its good sides, but you know, I've seen others, and in the end, one gets tired of the luxury … We'll speak more of it later … You must be dying of hunger, no?"

During this flood of words, the stranger fluffed my pillows and rearranged my sheets. Once he felt the bed was more inviting, he put down the tray on which sat a big pot of coffee whose aroma finally softened me up completely. I let none of this show: I kept my weapon aimed at the intruder.

I thus observed the strange gentleman who'd just entered my private space in a way that was both brutal and surreal.

The man fussing in front of me must have been at least 70 years old. His dark-complected face had numerous wrinkles and curvatures that only age can sculpt. Yet his somewhat round cheeks and soft features gave him a certain something that was decidedly youthful. No angle pared down the curves of his nose or his well-defined mouth. There was something gentle about him, although he was, as I quickly noticed, blind in one eye. Fairly tall, and gracefully slender, he wore his black hair—dyed perhaps—short and curly. A few artfully placed grey strands gave him a rather distinguished look. Dressed in jeans and a mostly unbuttoned white shirt, over which he had tied an immaculate starched apron, he wore an amused smile. His Hispanic accent endeared him to me, despite the strangeness of the situation. His impeccable French, almost precious in certain turns of phrase, contrasted with his voice's very Hispanic, practically caricatural modulations. He continued, seeing that I was readjusting the towel that I had tied around my hips. "Don't be embarrassed, I've seen others. I've come across a great many naked women in my life. And I loved them. But I couldn't care less about their bodies; I'm a homosexual. Homosexuals: It's a species that no longer exists, you know. Now everyone desires everyone. Bisexual, queer … Yes, queer. Or some such word … But me, I remain 100% homo. I'm the last of the Mohicans, and you cannot be as interesting to me as you are to the members of Echthros. A woman of your calibre, who's being protected so diligently and who must therefore still be very important to our ranks, must have noticed it, right? Did you make a big mistake? You seem more like the type who's led a truly massive and dangerous mission … You were sacrificed in some way. You were sent into an ambush, you did what you had to do, and now you're the one who pays. Don't answer. Do *not* answer! I'm just doing this to provoke you. To see if you're tempted to tell me everything. People are weak, especially in the morning before such a good breakfast. On an empty stomach, one is ready to squeal on everyone, even on friends and even on oneself … You mustn't … You're not being hidden like this for nothing. They don't want you to be tortured until you confess things to others or even to them … How do you take it?" he asked quickly as he indicated the coffee he was pouring for me.

How could this odd man be concerned about my specific preference in beverages while I was pointing my Sig Sauer in his direction? He remained unflappable, and I wondered if I should listen to his spiel, thanks to which, as I could already tell, he would eventually win me over.

"I have to learn … We're going to be living together, or almost … right? Milk? A little then. Sugar? No? Why not? It's better with sugar, the way the South Americans, the Greeks, and the Turks like it. You know nothing about coffee. You … You drink like a savage, like a European lady on a diet. Without sugar … I'm adding a tiny touch of sweetness, even if you don't want it … You'll get used to it, and in three months, you'll no longer do without it. You'll have become my soul sister, no longer the Organization's most disloyal rogue agent in the world … you're going to have to stop controlling your life. You'll eventually end up dying of an ulcer … You have to loosen up … But don't go thinking that you'll have nothing to do here, that you'll be served breakfast in bed every morning. Today you're getting the royal treatment—the VIP treatment, as they say in the hospitality business. Yes, alright. But the novelty will soon wear off! Oh! You ate the chocolate I left for you last night? You fell into my trap, my darling! Just as I expected! Quite the gourmand … You'd cave quickly under torture … All it would take is a piece of Ferrero Rocher or a bit of nougat. Still, you must learn to pick up the wrappers … Look, Saturna put a wastebasket in the corner. You'll like Saturna, that woman never speaks. Sometimes I think the enemies cut out her tongue … But no … That's just the way she is: discreet … Everything exists in this world, and every thing has its place. Even when it comes to trash. Aren't you the greedy one! And yet you're not that fat … really not. Fairly small breasts. You didn't want to get implants … Isn't that the latest fashion? You're thin. You must tell me your secret, my dear. You see, I've gained a few kilos due to stress and to all these people I take care of. Because you are not the only ones. I have two or three houses to manage. I spend my life running errands. How do you say 'safe houses' in French, damn it? I watch too many movies in English. I'm going to lose the language, and I spent so much time learning it. It'll be like we're in *La disparition de la langue française*, the novel by Assia Djebar. I'll tell you about that some other time. I remember the expression: *maison de protection rapprochée* … A close-protection house. I'm telling you, French is no simple matter, one can't take the easy way out. Lola, come, come, she's not a meanie, this flat-chested girl … Lola, don't be afraid to come into the room, yes, that's right …"

The man was speaking to a long-haired little dog that was hesitating to come toward me. She remained in the doorway, indecisive, wondering whether or not to bark. I still hadn't lowered my Sig Sauer. It was ridiculous, but I still didn't have confidence in this guy, even if everything about him tried to show me how wrong I was to distrust him. As for the so-called Lola, she hardly seemed reassured by weapons, whose existence she was clearly aware of. There was a very brief silence during which the man went to get his little dog, picking her up off the ground. I was able to regain my composure.

"You're Otto, right?" I asked firmly. My voice seemed inclined to intimidate the man in front of me.

"Otto? Humph! What an idea … Do I look like an Otto?" He thought for a minute and said with a laugh, "Ah! Of course! That's what they call me, those two big American broads, built like tanks. They were the ones who brought you here? I pretended to be an Otto; it had quite the effect on those nitwits. Otto … I even spoke to them in German. They believed it, with my Hispanic accent, and can you imagine, I lisp … They are illiterate, those beasts … Only seen movies about Nazis or CIA guys, it would appear. No chance to rise up through the ranks. Going to be prison guards, or something like that, their whole life. They could swallow you whole. Nothing like Lola … A distinguished little dog, don't you think? Don't you just want to cuddle up with her? Look how she likes your bed, now … She is nothing like the SS's she-wolf … No, I'm not Otto. *Nein* … For you, I'll be … I'll be … Celestino, I'm Titino, do you like the name? I chose it for you, for the occupants of your 'close-protection house' … But your group will not live in a house. It's a lovely apartment building, as you will see … I come from Cuba, like in a novel of this sort … you know the writer who committed suicide because he had AIDS. Reinaldo … Reinaldo Arenas. *Celestino antes del alba*, that's the title of the book. There was also a film based on an autobiography by Arenas, *Antes que anochezca*. Not bad. With Javier Bardem, gorgeous as a god when he was young. Lately, he's put on quite a lot of weight … a bit bloated, don't you think? You're not answering; it must depend on one's preferences. Thin as you are, you must look for a little extra fat on your men … or women. Like Garbo, I'm telling you … at least, that's the rumour … You've read the letters that she exchanged with Mercedes de Acosta, you know, the Cuban woman

... The correspondence is called *Here Lies the Heart*. In English ... I'm not completely losing my memory. So, in *Celestino*, Arenas's book, it's the narrator's cousin who becomes either a madman or a poet. He starts writing everywhere. You know him, don't you? A great writer ... As for me, I only reads books by homosexuals, I decided to do it like that because I was tired of stories by heteros ... You must have read it. You seem well-educated, little one. Uh ... what's your name? Don't answer. You wouldn't lie, not to me. That would be a serious mistake. Very, very serious ... I don't know the truth. But then, it's of so little interest to me. Don't be concerned. They didn't give me a file on you. I'm not supposed to know anything about your past. So you can invent, you can write your own novel ... Here, you can rewrite your life ... It's perfectly natural that I have no idea who you once were. Imagine ... if I ever betrayed our cause ...You don't trust me, and perhaps you have good reason not to. You mustn't trust anyone. Let me guess your name ... I'll make one up ... Something like Albertine ... Albertine, Proust's prisoner. No one knows more about books by homosexuals than I do, my dear. Fair warning. Yes, yes, I agree, Proust is not difficult and we're all familiar with Albertine. But even so. You're going to have to start reading or go back to reading because I hold literary contests for us ... It's a game, Celestino's game. I detest uneducated spies. And Lord knows, there are plenty of them. I told them at the Organization not to send me any ignoramuses. And surprise, surprise, they listened to me. And you, you look like you studied philosophy or literature, or maybe political science, before committing yourself to the cause. You're a scholar who's lost herself over the years. A long, long time ago, you weren't such a ninny, am I right? You seem to be worn out by your ardent devotion to Agathos."

I was touched by the comment that Celestino had just made about my weariness. I had been trained to ignore the sweet-talking of others, but the way this man had read me really hit close to home. And when he mentioned the lassitude that develops during a lifetime spent in the secret service, I felt exhausted by my past, despite the excellent night's sleep I'd just had.

"Well, I'm going to open the curtains wider, we need the bright light of day. It's good for the morale. I painted your room pale pink before you came. The colour goes with your sheets. In the dim light, one might think I put you all in white. But this is no hospital here. Hmm! I should have chosen a darker pink. This light pink is too deathly pale … I'll find you different sheets, okay … As I told you, they are ready to pay. As long as you behave. I knew nothing about you. All they told me was a woman. But I couldn't be sure that this was true. You know how they always throw you a red herring. As for us, we become inscrutable. We make sure that everything is all muddled up, so that those we converse with can't understand a thing … The pale pink isn't a bad choice, it gives you a heathy glow without ruining your skin tone … Look … It rained last night. The sky poured down us. But this morning, see how sunny it is, and your room is nice and bright before noon, despite what one might think. Don't frown, it'll give you wrinkles … There's no one right across from us, you have nothing to fear. And the cars out there can't see us because of the distance and the hedge that separates us from life. I've thought of absolutely everything. And now, I'm going to do your laundry. Only today. After this, you'll be your own maid. We'll have to order you some things. Saturna will come help you make a list of whatever toiletries you're missing. But I myself will order your clothes or will personally go buy them so that you'll be better dressed … I don't trust your sartorial choices. Creatures like you, you've disguised yourselves as normal people for far too long … You believe that you have to deck yourself out in some cookie-cutter uniform … You're not going to play Cinderella here, are you? There's no need. The Organization pays for propriety. You didn't have time to pick up your luggage? All my guests arrive the way you did. It's the Hotel Budapest way. The Grand Hotel Budapest way: with nothing. You have to recreate yourself here. You're the first one I'm visiting this morning. You're the queen in this apartment building. Queen Christine. Garbo, always Garbo … I put you in the prettiest room, the one that looks to the southeast. And yet I could have put a princess here. But I chose you, you'll see, you'll understand. You are my chosen one. I love these rooms, the southeasterlies, I call them. You're a lucky duck. You just don't realize it … Lola, stop barking at the dear lady and you, dear lady, put down your gun. Lola wants hugs, not a bullet in the brain. You can't quite make up your mind? Listen to me carefully, use a little logic, Bella. You could die if your coffee were poisoned. Although death would come instantly … But you could also trust me. Or you could kill yourself right now, big shot. Go ahead, your pistol will do the trick. Put a bullet in your brain. Saturna and I will clean up the mess. Lola will sniff your blood … You won't be the first … What do you want me to say? Would you like me to hide the truth from you. That's not my style. You have to decide. Between life with the old homo whom you don't trust and death. I speak French, don't I, Albertine? It's part of the job. You have to be multilingual. It makes so many things possible. Besides, one of my husbands was Vice-Consul of France before he was assassinated—perhaps, in fact, by me. No one ever knew. And I myself have forgotten … Come, Lola, come get acquainted. You have to get used to this naughty girl who loves her pistol the way a man loves his penis … They teach you how to become guys in the Organization, don't you agree? I'm going to turn you back into a woman."

He took the dog in his arms and put her in mine, thus forcing me to put down the gun. I had just yielded, capitulated … Happy that I could abandon myself to the sense of security that this stream of words brought me. Then Celestino began walking around the room to inspect and clean it up. To see what he might have missed.

"This is more like it. Lola in your arms … and the curtains open wide … Yes, this is good. Do you like pictures, posters, paintings, knick-knacks? I'll buy you some, when I know you better. If there's still someone inside you … I'm not so sure about it. Knock, knock, is there anyone inside this body? I don't think so. Your room needs a little decoration, too. Bare walls cause melancholia. I don't have a minimalist soul. I prefer kitsch. You'll find something to wear in the dresser, but the clothes might be a bit big for you. Stuff gets left in an apartment … I've collected some pretty things, things I'd wear if I were a young lass. No, I wouldn't be such an ostentationist. Can you say that in French? Have no fear. I can see the fear on your face. I'm not going to turn you into a drag queen."

He stopped his speechifying for a moment, put on a serious face, and continued as he pointed a finger at me. "You might not realize it, but you have so many prejudices against homosexuals that you're being ridiculous about it. You've read too many bad books, my child. And besides, you mustn't believe what's written in the literature. I didn't know that you're also not very tall. Nothing like the two monsters who brought you here last night … They should ask you about your diet. Those two balloons are about to burst … Ah! You're reading *The Diary of Anne Frank*!" he commented as he put my bag, from which the book stuck out, on a chair. "As it happens, Anne Frank had decorated her room with pictures of movie stars … Do you like celebrities? I doubt it. You're too intellectual to appreciate them. Your book is in German. Wait, wait. Then I should be playing the role of Anne's father Otto for you. Was his real name Otto, the one who survived, the only one to return from the camps? Otto … Follow his example, Albertine, follow the example of Otto who survived the war, not the example of that loser Anne Frank who didn't have what it takes to stay alive. A lightweight. A bit like you, I'm afraid … Anne Frank … Her diary. That's all we needed! This is not the right sort of reading for a recluse like you, for Marcel's prisoner, for Albertine, for Greta … it's all a little too gloomy. You must be entertained. There's no going out for fresh air here. But you're allowed to do everything else. There's the television in the big common room. And the Internet in one office. Do note, however, that you don't have access to everything. Surely you understand why, but there are things to do. You'll have to handle some household chores and play with Lola, who eventually gets bored with a man as busy as I am. And besides, she likes only young people, the little minx, like women! She can't abide the smell of old age: That's why I have a big loofah to get rid of the epidermal layers that reek of old age. I'll buy you one if you'd like. You seem a little masochistic, like your Anne Frank. You must like to scrub yourself with a loofah … How old are you, my sweet … 40, 45? Hard to say. This morning, you look haggard, and you're having a very bad hair day. You'll fix yourself up in the bathroom mirror. I see that you're not wearing any nail polish. You're wrong, it's cheerier when your hands are done. My mother couldn't bear it if her finger- and toenails weren't polished. She used to say that without polish, her limbs looked like they were in mourning. She prayed God that she'd still have red polish when she lay in her grave. But here, you'll have lots of time for things of that sort. You'll be able to take care of yourself and your soul, something you've neglected since your student days. You've been running and running, for how long? Too long? The Grand Hotel Budapest is offering you a rejuvenating experience. You'll take care of yourself here. Like Hans Castorp in *The Magic Mountain*. See, I know only homosexuals' literature, and don't try to tell me that Thomas Mann wasn't 'that way.' It's because you haven't read his diary, have you?"

Like me, Celestino had thought of Mann's book to describe the situation in which we found ourselves. I might have been surprised, but I was too hungry. This fellow seemed capable of entering other people's psyche, and I had to be wary. I would ponder this later—I had the time. As a response to the questions posed by my host, who in fact had not asked me for any commentary at all, I greedily devoured the croissants and sank my teeth into the chocolate Danishes. It felt so good to eat! Over the years, I had learned not to overly enjoy food anymore. I had been wrong. I got back an appetite I hadn't hoped to have again.

Celestino was already pushing me out of bed so that he could more easily make it. As I stood there practically naked, he urged me to finish my breakfast. My mouth still full, I said, "Tell me, Otto, we're in Montreal, right?"

Without seeming to, I observed his smallest gestures and reactions to determine whether or not he would tell me the truth. He didn't answer right away. He seemed preoccupied by something else. He simply said, "Tomorrow, I want you to make your bed by yourself. These are the first things to do in the morning. You understand? You get up, you make your bed. This is how you join the world. We have a ritual that says: 'Yes, I am here, I am awake.'" He went into the bathroom to see what I'd done during the night, upon my arrival, and managed to exclaim, "But you cannot leave the towels on the floor, my dear. This is not a pigsty. How did your mother raise you? In Havana, my own mother slapped me on the back of my head or kicked my ass if I didn't do such things properly ... And when it came to matters of grooming, she was uncompromising. She trained me."

I interrupted him. I had just remembered where I'd heard that comment about beds to be made. At boarding school, certainly, but also in a book.

"You've read Duras? Marguerite Duras? She made her bed every morning, it was important to her. A way to start the day, no matter what happens, but you didn't answer the question I asked about the city we're in."

Celestino said nothing at first, then finally replied angrily, "Do not speak to me of that execrable female, who despised homos but lived with a goddamn pedophile. I can't stand her; she writes very badly ... I forbid you to speak to me about that floozy who won the Goncourt on top of everything else ... I prefer Yourcenar over her. Among the French women ... If one must like French women ... Well, fine ... I assumed that on this point, we wouldn't agree, were we to discuss it ... but I don't want to. We'll have enough topics on which to disagree!" Without catching his breath, he promptly exclaimed, "Montreal! Why not ... Yes, we're in Montreal, yes, yes, if you believe so. In Paris, if you'd like. Or in Rome, if that's what you imagine. Here, we're wherever we want to be. It's the Hotel Budapest, located in the imaginary Republic of Zubrowka. You don't recognize it? You're lying; you haven't seen the film, that's for sure! You can watch it in the living room. When I was a child, my parents owned an immense hotel in Cuba, where we hosted the country's intelligentsia. Later, when I was a young man, the Russians came ... They were sophisticated people with whom I learned to make a bed, arrange a tray, eat caviar, dance the waltz, and knock back bottles of vodka. And they also taught me how to train dogs. Lola, she learned everything from me. She was raised the Russian way. Vaganova Method for dogs." And he performed an impressive plié and relevé, to show me that he had followed the ballet techniques of the great Agrippina from Saint-Petersburg. He instantly made me think of my grandmother, who had been a dancer and had made of game of practicing pliés in first, second, and third position.

I stood up, half-naked, and executed a balletic curtsy ... Celestino laughed. These associations of personal thoughts that enabled me to link my host to my family gave me, in spite of myself, some hope. They amused and reassured me. I could believe that I actually was in Montreal. The perfect place for pliés and relevés … Celestino continued, brushing the air with little jetés that he performed quickly with his legs. I imitated him, as I had done with my grandma when I was young.

"At first, Lola was a grubby little thing. Like you … I'll bring you to heel … Ah! That was a beautiful time in Cuba, the 1960s; I don't know why I've always worked with the public since then, even for Agathos, and I still do. I have a gift for languages, you see. This talent certainly had to serve some purpose. I could've become a dancer. Perhaps I was one. Who knows? I won't tell you, will I? Here, we must not remember the days gone by. And you, we don't need to ask you why you're here: you were suicidal, you were reading Nietzsche, nihilism and death tempted you. The guys or the gals from the Organization, they came to recruit you. In the beginning, you thought it was a wonderful idea, and exciting! Like in the New Wave movies you watched. Goodness, you were pretentious, young lady! Yes, of course, it's obvious. Afterward, you told yourself it would be a good way to die, and for some 20 or 25 years, you've thought of nothing else. You're no longer a snob, you read less or only in secret because you deny yourself the books you love … You draw your weapon and live with Anne Frank. You call that an existence … What could you do with your PhD in philosophy or literature or political science, Albertine, my Titine? Might as well be a secret agent, right … There's no future for people who think. Might as well learn to kill, eh, Albertine …"

The man was making me dizzy. Many of the things he was suggesting were awakening a joy I hadn't felt in a very long time. He was certainly very charming and seemed to be a real conversationalist. Yet I felt a bit resistant to the idea of sharing my morning and eventually the months or even years to come with this very shrewd fellow, this Titino, who didn't stop talking, who had "real smarts," as my grandmother used to say, and who would, no doubt, quickly end up getting on my nerves. He filled the space with his jetés and relevés. However, he did make me laugh, and I hadn't been able to have much fun lately. Nor had I known many people with whom I could easily converse over the past few years. So, I lied and replied, "You're way off base, Otto el Titino Grande, I don't have a degree in philosophy, or in social sciences. I'm just licensed to kill. That's it. I have no past, no future, no nothing. Your 'Neetch,' or whatever you call him? I don't know who that is. But you can call me Albertine or Titine or Greta; I prefer your inventions to my real name, which I left in an airport trash can along with my old weapon. Anne Frank, you're right, it's not much fun ... Something 'gayer' is better, to please old guys like you. But you have books here," I said, indicating the little bookcase that, the night before, I'd promised myself I would explore. "I could educate myself and play the scholar with you. I'm going to take another shower, my friend, and today, you're going to show me the premises or I'll tour the property on my own instead. Your Hotel Budapest looks to me like a rat hole. That's what I thought: a rundown rat hole. This place is no Ritz. I'm used to suites in palaces, so you can't fool me. But hey, I'm no longer entitled to the world's five-star hotels, any more than I am to luxury bars. We're in Montreal, that I know. Those two fine ladies let it slip. Their flab comes from Schwartz's, where they go to stuff their faces. I recognize the blubber that comes from smoked-meat. You know, I'm from here. When I was little, my family must have lived not too far from where we are. It's a curious coincidence, wouldn't you say?"

Celestino looked at me, incredulous. He laughed as he said, "And this one here, Lola, is not very amenable to us. You'll have to be careful, my angel, this little Titine is as formidable as the narrator's Titine. But Lola has seen others. We work with all clientèles. And since the days of my big hotel in Cuba, nothing has surprised me ... Montreal, it's a beautiful city, isn't it? A bit cold in the winter, a bit hot in the summer. Look out the window, and you'll see very well whether the climate here matches your memories. But with your imagination, you'll be able to live in your fantasy world. I bet that you did study literature after all. Yes, Montreal, why not?"

Celestino picked up the tray and adjusted the folds of the bedsheets, adding, "I'll be leaving with Lola, you're right, go see the property by yourself. This afternoon or this evening, I'll show you what you need to know, but from now until then, you're free."

He stuck his head into the bathroom to say goodbye or to see whether I was showering properly, without splashing water on the floor. This guy was a neat freak. It wouldn't be easy to play absent-minded with him. Everything must remain in its place. I called out to him from behind my pink shower curtain: "More importantly, *The Celestina* is the title of a tragicomedy written in Spain in the 15th Century. And Picasso also took inspiration from that story for his painting, *Celestina*, produced during his Blue Period. It shows an old woman, a cruel matchmaker who you remind me of ... She's blind in one eye, like you. You're Celestina, right? No, I don't know if I should trust you, Titino ... But my erudition will impress you, and you too will learn to be wary of your Titine. Celestina ... Doesn't that earn me some points for the games and contests that I assume we all have to participate in to keep you amused? You're someone who needs entertainment, Celestino, entertainment that is not always wholesome ... Me, not so much ... So I'm more patient than you and more focused on my target. I bet you I'm going win first prize in your contests, I just feel it!"

The only response I heard was the sound of the door to my room softly closing.

Chapter 4

I had just opened a can of Coke and was cutting a slice of tomato to tuck into my sandwich when I spotted the aristocratic old lady from *Mumu*. She was standing just behind me in the doorway.

It had been a long time since I'd read Turgenev's short story, written during his detention in a Saint Petersburg prison, but the character of the lady, an old dame as I remembered her, still remained quite vivid even after all these years. I must say that she was a royal bitch, that woman! She had viciously ruined the life of her serfs, especially that of Gerasim, when she made the woman he was madly in love with marry another man, a miserable old drunk. And then on a whim, perhaps to make Gerasim even more unhappy, she had ordered the death of his dog Mumu, who barked too much.

I had retained an appalling impression of this arrogant, rich woman, and when I learned that Ivan Sergeyevich Turgenev had chosen his own mother as the model for this shrew, I somehow felt comforted. This character had actually existed before inhabiting the story in which the poor creature, Mumu, met her death. I would have been devastated if Turgenev had birthed such a diabolical being by drawing her straight from his imagination. It always seemed to me—though it's debateable—that fiction is always much less cruel and malicious than reality. Writers' fabrications, like the worst nightmares, remain less traumatic than our civilizations' demented manifestations.

An old woman was growing impatient behind me. She was bouncing from one foot to the other. I hadn't yet seen her face nor had she opened her mouth, but I already loathed her. Earlier that morning, Celestino had, either intentionally or unintentionally, awakened my literary memories with his ridiculous game of naming each individual according to the fictional roles they embodied. And this imperious lady whom I did not know irritated me as much as any detestable character.

With an obvious and predictable air of reproach, which I saw as I turned around, the old lady asked me when I intended to bring them their meal. She and her husband had been waiting since morning. Because of the time difference, they'd eaten their breakfast very early. They were ravenous, and I hadn't even set the table yet!

The lady from *Mumu* was fairly tall and strong; her hair held in place by a wide headband covering her ears, her flowered blouse, and her black pants that seemed too warm for the climate gave her an old-fashioned look that fit with my image of Turgenev's old woman.

Despite the conversation's excessively domestic turn, I was still a bit nervous to sense someone I didn't know right there, so close, in front of me. I was already regretting having made the reckless decision to go to the kitchen without my gun. That very morning, I'd convinced myself to trust the safety measures that Celestino and his bosses had established in the Annex. The coming days and months would likely be unliveable if I continued to remain on guard. And when I heard Mumu the dog's assassin expound on her own timetable and on her appetite, I understood that the good woman was not putting my life in danger. However, my pistol was going to become a weapon to be turned on myself once I'd spent three months with this pain in the ass.

Like me, she'd just arrived, and she was surprised to find herself in this place. She was from a Slavic country that had once been part of the USSR. Her accent was proof of this, but she had never worked as a secret agent. That was as plain as day. She was there because of her husband, whose life she followed ...

To better understand these people and thereby keep them at a distance, I was going to have to consider their former life. I really didn't want to, but alas, living together left little opportunity for isolation and solitude. This is true of annexes in every era and in every conceivable place. *The Diary of Anne Frank* had again shown this to be true just this morning. The passages about the quarrels between Mrs. van Pels (rechristened van Daan in the book) and Anne's mother had seemed quite enlightening on this subject. The two women in the Annex did nothing but squabble. Little Anne had spent many days detesting her father, her mother, her sister, Pfeffer the dentist (alias Albert Dussel), as well as the van Pels family.

Communal living is definitely unbearable.

I had joyfully immersed myself in Anne Frank's words right after my shower, postponing my inspection of the Annex, which I knew would prove to be a banal apartment building. Celestino had undoubtedly set everything up so that I would lead the most normal life possible. The spaces had been designed to ensure that my integration went smoothly. Unlike Anne Frank, I had thus put off visiting my new home. I hadn't undertaken any tidying-up activities. Instead, I'd opted for indolence, and I'd begun this magnificent Montreal day in my room with my book.

The sun came through the wide-open window. During her adolescence in Montreal, my mother must have spent the summer in the city's humidity. Even today, it was terribly hot, but I found it pleasant. I had stayed glued to my sheets, in my sweat, until sometime after noon. Hunger had pulled me from my reader's lethargy, and I had decided to go see if there was something for me in the refrigerator. Just before that, I had taken yet another shower, attempting to halt for a moment the perspiration project my body had been working on since the previous night. The water was nice and refreshing. It was the second time that day that I was bathing. It had been a little indulgence. I realized that I was already developing a few habits. I was settling in … Was this a good sign? I didn't know. I got dressed, feeling refreshed but still grumbling about the Organization, which hadn't given a damn about supplying us with air conditioners. But in Montreal, the summer heat waves would be short-lived. I would soon find heating more essential than cool air.

As Celestino had assured me, my room was at the back of the apartment building. It faced the south-east, and so I had sunlight for part of the afternoon. Noises from the Annex didn't reach me. The very long hallway, which I had taken the previous night with my two guard dogs to reach my room, was flanked by six rooms, three on either side. I set out without knowing exactly where to go, and I quickly saw that two of the doors to these rooms were open. The mattresses were bare, a bit forlorn without sheets. No one was occupying these quiet rooms yet. Only a cat, stretched out on a chest of drawers, seemed to be keeping watch from his perch over the comings and goings of people like me who were venturing out to discover the Annex. He kept his eye on me and seemed to smile at me the way the Cheshire Cat in *Alice in Wonderland* might have. How could this beautiful animal get along with Celestino's Lola? I continued my tour. The fifth and sixth doors just at the end of the corridor remained closed. The rooms they protected from my inquiring eyes must have already been taken by new arrivals like me.

It was my understanding that the Annex had just been invaded by its new occupants. The previous night, it had received a group of new arrivals. This explained why I had originally believed the apartment was empty. However, I gathered from my first moments in the hallway that once we (I was already saying "we" as if Celestino's protégés were destined to become a community; I knew that no matter what I did, I'd end up saying "we") were all there, the Annex would seem jam-packed. A far cry from Anne Frank's living conditions. Yet with all these people near me, my life was not likely to be a barrel of laughs. I'd led a solitary life for many years. In fact, after boarding school, I had never again shared my living space. Even at university, I rented myself a small apartment where I lived without a roommate. After my college years, lack of privacy disgusted me. How could I possibly live with a bunch of people again?

Just past the rooms, a big kitchen on the left side of the hallway bade me come satisfy my hunger. Celestino, ever the attentive host, had not failed to leave me food to eat. He made seeing to every detail such a point of honour. He or Saturna must have gone shopping and filled the pantry with groceries. Saturna … Saturna … Wasn't that the name of Tristana's housemaid in the book by Benito Pérez Galdós? It had been more than 25 years since I'd opened a work written by the Spanish author of historical realism, which in fact I didn't care for at all back then. And yet I remembered the servant's name in that old novel! My memory was certainly faithful. Yes, the housekeeper must be a modern version of Pérez Galdós's Saturna. I would speak to Celestino to set the record straight.

I was just about to enter the kitchen when I saw a very bright light coming from what I immediately understood to be an enormous room. The hallway actually made a sharp turn and opened into a very large living room attached to an imposing dining room. The common spaces in this apartment would quickly compel us to share our lives, to live in very close quarters that I found quite undesirable, and that would eventually require confinement to my room. Shelves of books covered the room's walls from top to bottom. At least there would be something to read … Perhaps *Tristana* could be found among the rows of books. Celestino knew how to keep us busy, and I had also realized that he liked to toy with us. He was obviously making me live with intellectuals. These people might distract me from my former acquaintances. The Organization must have thought there was an effective way to compartmentalize its employees in the various annexes it felt obliged to establish: their level of education, their culinary preferences, their passion for sports, or their skills with cutting-edge technology. How could its members be assigned to a single house?

Beyond the living-dining room, there was a smaller but very respectable space in which two large sofas and a gigantic television battled for centre stage. The room as a whole looked like a sitting room; it too intended to accommodate the entire household for times when we'd all be together …

As I left the living room where I had no wish to linger, I noticed other rooms. I decided to check them out later. I was hungry and very likely had plenty of time to get used to the premises. The kitchen awaited. I thought it looked very nice, sparkling clean with its numerous electrical appliances. There was enough here to cook several feasts a day. We were apparently expected to serve ourselves, to become men and women more concerned with comfort, cooking, and food than with the possibility of our own assassination. A feeling of well-being would make us forget that we were afraid to be here, confined together *ad vitam æternam*, so close to death.

As expected, I'd found a full and extremely well-organized refrigerator from which I'd taken a lovely loaf of bread and a ripe tomato to make myself a sandwich. I'd also found a big jar of mayonnaise in a cupboard. Coke was the drink I'd settled on. It had been years since I'd last had one. It seemed important to celebrate the moment by doing something slightly incongruous. Our lives are locked into foolish little habits that give us a personality. These ridiculous behaviours build a framework that supports our feeble reasons to live. As an agent on the Agathos payroll, I'd tried to erase such idiosyncrasies only to adopt others in an arbitrary, haphazard fashion, but I'd only managed to invent a different me, as insignificant as the one that my history or even my genetics had created. A Coke tempted me, and I wasn't going to deny myself the pleasure. Not anymore, not in the Annex.

The lady from *Mumu* was growing impatient in the kitchen because I wasn't answering her. Her English began to deteriorate. She stammered. Right off the bat, I addressed her in Russian, saying that despite what she might have thought, I was not the maid. I doubted that there was even someone there to serve her. Surprised that I knew her language, the old woman smiled, twisting her lips into some sort of benevolent, condescending grimace. She did, however, seem very perplexed. It seemed hard for her to believe that no one present was ready to submit to her desires. She cited the name of the servant that the guesthouse's proprietor (as she called Celestino) had mentioned earlier that morning. So I don't answer to the name Saturna? What a shame. Yet she had believed it to be so; she'd been wrong and found that confusing. She and her husband had sat at the little table that had been provided for them in their room, and they waited to receive at least a tray with sandwiches and scones, as is customary in British countries. But now she understood that nothing had been prepared, that Saturna was clearly someone other than me, and that she'd have to serve herself. She coyly added in English so as to be clearly understood by all those who might be there but whom she did not see, that she was an excellent cook. No doubt she would be able to do the food more justice than a kitchen maid or a Saturna ever could. This she said with a strange look, that of a woman from another time who wants to remain modest but knows the value of her assets. Her tone conveyed the deep conviction that her roast veal and her quiche had amazed all of her husband's guests. That was how she had been appreciated and cherished in the past.

I saw her rummaging in the refrigerator, vexed but determined to make the best of a bad situation. I finished my sandwich, thinking that I wouldn't stay there long. But since the kitchen was large and had room for a long counter with silver stools, I sat a while to devour my tomato washed down with Coke. What a treat! It had been ages since I'd tasted anything so good! Old Mumu was trying to remember a familiar dish that she could make with the ingredients—mediocre, in her opinion—found in the refrigerator. I was right: She came from an era when a girl had to learn how to bake a cake for important occasions, with rose water or orange blossom and saffron threads. That's how women like her found a rich husband whose money meant that they'd never have to cook a day in their life.

I was wondering whether I should make myself two more sandwiches, since I was still so hungry, when I saw a man hesitating at the door of the kitchen. He was fairly stooped and must have been 80 years old. He greeted me from a distance and, both fearful and imperious, spoke to his wife in Russian without entering the kitchen, which was an unsuitable place for a person of his rank and sex. He asked her what time he might finally eat and what she was fumbling for in the refrigerator. He didn't know if he should introduce himself to the woman perched on the stool voraciously eating a sandwich. His manners dictated that he should approach me, but the startling situation in which he found himself no longer allowed him to rely on the habits of his excellent upbringing. This man looked nothing like a spy! Despite having the scornful attitude of the well-to-do, these two old people had nothing to do with the secret service. To comprehend how they'd ended up in the Annex, you'd have to assume that they'd been tools used by the Organization. Because of their social situation or their influence, they had served the Government and were now caught in an international ambush that they had presumably not expected and from which they could never escape alive, considering their age. They would be obliged to hide out until they died, like common thieves, at least that's what they must have been thinking.

I might have felt some pity for them had the woman not immediately made me think of Turgenev's evildoer and had the old man not reminded me, as he spoke to his wife in a pompous tone, of the retired general in *Two Landowners*, another one of Turgenev's extraordinary short stories—by which I mean a haughty and foolish man, sort of an old playboy, pretentious with his subordinates and enmeshed in intricacies and convoluted nonsense with his superiors. It was surely his fawning, meticulous manners toward slightly higher-ranking people that led to their downfall, both his and his wife's. Someone he considered to be important had called, asking him in a grandiloquent way to participate in a coup essential to the country's—the world's—proper functioning … This popinjay hadn't been able to refuse; he'd believed in the decisive role he had to play by helping keep the planet safe and secure. He was simply going to spend the rest of his life in the Annex, dragging his wife with him into a life of deprivation. More aware of her rank, she would never have agreed to submit to an underling. The supplications of an ignorant bureaucrat would have actually convinced her not to take action. She was a strong-willed woman who had killed a dog and made a manservant suffer whenever she had the chance. Although she and her husband both proved susceptible to flattery, she—like a Turgenev character—knew how to stand strong in certain circumstances. But she'd married a wimp and now in her old age had to endure it. When she arrived at the Annex, she entered a different novel, one that hadn't been written for her. She knew neither its plot nor its dialogues. Of course, she would cope for a while. But the anger and bitterness that her situation would arouse would not be directed against her husband. The Annex's residents would very soon suffer Mumu's vexations, and I would have to keep my distance from the dear lady. I would quickly inform her that she should find someone other than me to be her scapegoat. I had been friends with an old couple during my last mission, and I had very bad memories of that. The Turgenevs weren't for me …

As I swallowed the last bite of the sandwich I'd made, I decided to say hello, without any qualms and with my mouth full, to the gentleman of the Turgenev couple who, flabbergasted, gave me another quick nod of the head and withdrew to the living room, where he leafed through a book while waiting for his wife. He walked slowly. He dragged his feet in fur slippers that were highly inappropriate for the very warm weather we were experiencing. Madame Mumu had plunged her head into the refrigerator, continuing to search its drawers without finding anything that she could prepare. Once she stood back up, distraught over not knowing what to do, she quickly spotted on the counter the loaf of bread that I'd already started. After a very brief moment of hesitation, she asked me in Russian where this miraculous item had come from. She dared not humble herself by asking me for a slice and hoped that I would find in a kitchen cabinet a whole loaf reserved in her name. I hastily got up, picked up the knife lying beside the bread, promptly cut her six thin slices, and took the opportunity to make myself one more sandwich. Mumu barely thanked me. To her near-sighted eyes, the honour was entirely mine. She was having difficulty resigning herself to the fact that I was not her slave.

Living with Russian aristocrats would not be easy … They were going to play the Slav during their entire stay here and put on sad, melancholy faces to demonstrate their deprivation, of which they alone could take full measure. No one could comprehend the luxury in which they'd spent their life or how hard it was to end up in Celestino's guest house after having lived such a fabulous existence. As for me, I thought that the Turgenevs might spoil my time at the Annex. I was already comparing the gentleman to the dentist with whom Anne had shared her room. However, I preferred to call them the Turgenevs rather than the Pfeffers. It seemed more accurate, historically and culturally. "Turgenev" seemed to be the perfect last name for people who, like a good number of the characters in the Russian novelist's writings, regretted that the world had changed and that educated rich folk were no longer the masters of the universe.

Celestino was not going to appreciate this sobriquet, and he would be annoyed by my references to Turgenev, that old hetero. He was going to forbid me to think of authors who loved women or their bodies, even though he himself must not have deprived himself of this very pleasure with Benito Pérez Galdós's Saturna. Yes, he would scold me. Unless he managed to come up with some cockamamie story about Turgenev's hidden homosexuality. After all, the Russian writer had been friends with Flaubert, who became a queer icon in the 1980s with his closeted homosexual adventures. Letters proved that Flaubert was not who we thought he was. Why not imagine that Celestino and Turgenev had had a casual love affair or even that they'd based their relationship on the Greek model? In truth, I was fairly eager to see Celestino again and to see how he would react upon hearing the Turgenevs' baptismal name. He would also explain Saturna to me.

I was a bit troubled by my feelings about Celestino. The damn Cuban seemed rather crafty. He had spoken to me only once, and already my thoughts drew me toward him. He had awakened me from a deep sleep earlier that morning and had also awakened in me the literature that had lain dormant for years. This was no small feat ... But instead of surrendering myself to a banal and benign consolation in this budding relationship, I knew I had to be suspicious: I could, unwittingly, find myself caught in my jailer's nets. What stratagem had he planned for me? Celestino said he knew nothing about me and was guessing at everything. In fact, he may even have intentionally talked to me about novels. After having read my file, which he claimed he had *not* read, he had doubtlessly learned how to start a conversation with me and to manipulate me. When I was young, I had lived through and for books, and if there was one sacrifice I'd made when changing my life, it was giving up literature. But now, thanks to the diabolical Celestino in this Annex-cum-library, books would again be my true companions. I would be able to reconnect with the person I'd once been. Hard to imagine that it all stemmed from an ordinary coincidence. Even harder to believe that Titino had formulated a Machiavellian scheme to entrap me. For the moment, I decided to put off drawing a conclusion on the subject of Celestino. I thought instead about *Kiss of the Spider Woman, El beso de la mujer araña*, that wonderful novel by the Argentinian author, Manuel Puig. In it, Molina betrays Valentin, with whom he shares a prison cell. I banish the thought. It wasn't yet time to panic.

I was mulling over these thoughts as I washed the dishes, which Madame Mumu found enormously annoying. Apparently she needed the sink to make her tomato sandwiches, since this most excellent cook had decided to copy my meal … I was blocking her way. At least that's what she tried to convey to me without deigning to ask me to move aside. There we were, wordlessly fighting each other using nothing but the choreography of our enemy bodies to gain access to the water, when a young man entered the dining room, yelling in French: "I'm taking my shower, you idiot! With you squandering the hot water, I have nothing but cold … Stop it this instant!" The young man, who must have been perhaps 25 years old, was wearing a big bathrobe that he'd found somewhere or other. Foaming shampoo ran down his rather dark-skinned face, making his presence almost theatrical.

Since I wasn't moving, he approached me, and with a surprising resoluteness considering the clothing he wore, he turned off the tap, horrifying Madame Mumu, who understood that her turn at the sink would unfortunately be delayed. Her husband would eventually get impatient, and this undoubtedly made her very nervous. And then she silently wondered who'd had the ludicrous idea to put her in a guest house with an impolite woman who stuffed herself with sandwiches and a young fellow who paraded through the kitchen with soap suds on his head. I myself felt like killing this guy who was too aggressive for my taste and who had entered my life and my corner of the sink without so much as a warning. But he left the room where we all were so quickly to go back to a bathroom, which I gathered was right next door, that for a second I stood there dumbstruck. Who was I on my way to becoming? I hadn't heard the water running a short distance away; I hadn't leapt at the young man's throat. Obviously, I had already lowered my guard and lost some of my instincts as an observer of the world, which my work had required for more than 20 years … Now, instead of listening for the slightest odd sound, I was losing myself in Turgenev and Puig, imagining that I was speaking to one of Reinaldo Arenas's characters, the malevolent Celestino. And then, already at fault, I didn't even defend myself when the shower guy attacked. This hideout was likely to transform me, and I was worried about the situation. Because I badly needed my abilities as a secret agent. The Turgenevs would not come to my rescue if I were in danger. In a novel, Ivan Turgenev himself, the great painter of souls, would merely have had a kind thought upon the death of people like me, but he never would have lifted a single finger to help me.

I turned the water back on and finished doing my dishes. This time, I listened to the young man's voice coming through the walls, calling me a bitch in French. He threatened me with the worst during the coming years in the Annex and intended to have me thrown out of there by Celestino over whom, he boasted from his shower, he had a certain influence.

I made myself some coffee, letting the water run. The old woman watched me in fear, without truly understanding what was happening. Her husband, upon hearing the racket the young man was making, had decided to return to the kitchen to see what had become of his meal. The old gentleman entered the room at the same time as the young fellow, who had still managed to finish washing and dress in a tee shirt, beige pants, and white tennis shoes that sparkled with cleanliness. He was walking straight toward me, intending to yell at me or threaten me, when I grabbed from Mumu's hands the knife she'd been using to slice onions and picked up a big chunk of juicy tomato, all in one fell swoop. I went toward the man, brandishing my weapons—the tomato and the knife—and said, "In my line of work, I am not accustomed to being insulted, and I've knocked off a fair number of guys bigger and braver than you. You're gonna stop your chariot right there, Ben Hur! You're going to stop acting this way, or you'll find yourself slaughtered or strangled in your shower. Like in Hitchcock's *Psycho*. You know the scene … Despite your youth … We're stuck here. We're going to remain civilized. I'd be happy to stop running the hot water, but you have to ask nicely, you snot-nosed little brat. You could mention respect for the environment instead of respect just for yourself. How was anyone to know you were busy performing your ablutions in the bathroom? You must communicate … See? You act nice, you don't play the diva, and everything will be fine … Otherwise, it'll be war between us, and I'd advise you against that. I won't mess up your sneakers with my tomato this time … Say thank you … I'm 45 years old and don't have my whole life ahead of me. I'm not afraid of death. But you are … It shows right away … You tell yourself that it would be a pity for a handsome dude like you to die so young … Me, I think otherwise. I also know that you're going to dream of murdering me in my sleep or strangling me from behind … You scream and yell, but you're a hypocrite. So, we become buddies, we forget, and you go back to being polite, otherwise we play at seeing who kills the other first or at who ruins your sneakers, and I warn you that I am highly regarded within the Organization as a wrecker of lives and sweet new kicks …"

The Turgenevs beat a hasty retreat, keeping their eyes on the floor. They remained silent as they waited for the young man to respond. And he, as I had expected, did not say a word. He tossed off a placated "Okay," which he meant to sound jaunty, but which still reeked of resentment. He quickly tried to speak to Madame Mumu, offering to make sandwiches with her. He even bragged that he knew how to concoct a little mayonnaise that she and her husband would adore. She accepted, terrified at first, then thrilled to have found a Frenchman at her disposal. Everything was falling into place. Madame Turgenev would have a servant. His lordship went back to the living room, not without giving me a dirty look, indicating that he disapproved of my bad manners and blamed me for what was happening to him. It was because of people like me—barbarians, philistines—that he and his wife had ended up in this guest house where the meal was not even served at midday.

The young man was chatting with Mumu. From my perch on the stool where I'd decided to sit back down, drink my coffee, and smoke a cigarette while intimidating my companions in misfortune who dared not deny me anything at all, I saw the young man take a knife from a drawer to cut the bread. He definitely thought for a few seconds about the opportunity he had to carve me up right there in the kitchen. But after a brief moment of reflection during which he must have remembered that his impetuous behaviour was the cause of his imprisonment in the Annex, he did not attack me. He wanted to appear docile and determined to obey.

But just where did he come from? A young man who wanted hot water for his shower, in the middle of a heat wave, who threw a tantrum and then capitulated the minute someone raised his voice: Was this the modern-day secret agent? Why was Agathos protecting this spineless guy who fluttered around Madame Mumu, complimenting her on the shape of her sandwiches? Was he really trying to start a conversation with me about the heat and the coffee's aroma? Who was this man-child? How did he come to be among us? He'd done something stupid on impulse … Zero self-control, that was obvious. But why had he been recruited in the first place? Had he assassinated one of our own? Had they arranged for him to liquidate someone inconvenient within the Organization? Was he a double agent? This nervous, hot-headed, boastful guy who trafficked in hate and vengeance reminded me of someone. Yes … But of whom? A boy I clearly didn't like … Charles Morel! Yes, Charles Morel, Proust's character, Baron Charlus's protégé. Celestino was going to be very proud of me for having recognized this young punk as a paper person invented by the greatest of homosexuals. Here I am in the presence of this petty, disagreeable man. He had tried to desert during the war in 1914 and had then succeeded in denouncing traitors while cloaking himself in his own moral virtue. Charles Morel, the coward who trembled in fear that his lover the baron would kill him, while he himself committed horrible acts of violence against his entourage. Charles Morel, who enjoyed torturing women but who played the gigolo with men. The ultimate parasite, a Lucien de Rubempré, only a little more gutless. What a character for a double agent! But how could the Organization have trusted him? Had it, from the outset, used his weaknesses for a despicable assignment? Were there readers of Proust in our secret service who sought Charles Morels to act as spies? I was almost forgetting the talents of Proust's character. As a violinist, he had received the conservatory's first prize. He also knew how to mingle with society folk and make them fall in love with him. And more importantly, he had made it to the end of his life having passed for a fine gentleman, a man of the greatest integrity.

My own Charles must also have been a cunning devil. He was wrapping Madame Turgenev around his little finger, and she was already simpering as she tasted his "yummy sandwich," and soon he'd start in on her husband. Maybe he'd sleep with both of the oldsters, making sure that neither of the Turgenevs confessed his infidelity to the other. He was telling Mumu the story about a famous woman, a certain Natacha, who was actively being sought by the enemy's secret service. She had just escaped an assassination attempt in broad daylight, and she was on every TV station. She had seduced the Russian president, spying on him for years. She had even married him. She worked for us even though outwardly, she was a member of England's royal family. She was Elizabeth's first cousin twice removed or something like that, and she was going to live at the Annex! Celestino had told Charles that Mata Hari would be here, among the members of our little gang, in a few hours, and Morel was squirming with impatience ... He needed company. He and Mumu were thrilled that such a wonderful woman would be joining us, rejoicing at the thought of welcoming a future housemate.

They seemed to have forgotten my existence, but from my seat on the stool, I interjected, "But the fact that this woman is going to be here in our apartment, among us (I had trouble saying this 'us,' but I was getting used to my affiliation with this repugnant community), is not good news ... Are you imbeciles or what? Every enemy's secret service is on her tail. If your story is true, the Russian president will not stop looking for his traitorous lover until she's dead. And when they find her, who else do you think they'll come across? All of us! You didn't think that, did you!?"

I was angry when I realized that Celestino and his friends in the Organization had housed me with these morons. But I was perhaps even more outraged to learn that they were going to stick us with Mata Hari, the most wanted woman on the planet. There was only one conclusion to be drawn: Agathos wanted us dead. We were expendable.

The four current occupants of this lovely apartment, this week's arrivals—myself, the two Turgenevs, and Charles—formed a pretty ridiculous group, and certainly an ineffective one should an Echthros commando manage to locate us. He would make quick work of these cowards, these mental cripples, these characters from old-fashioned novels. And me with my literary reminiscences, I was hardly much better. I was going to end up weakening over time. I already didn't recognize myself anymore. Everything to please a one-eyed old man! Fortunately, my altercation with the young guy and the old biddy reassured me. I was still able to keep people from pushing me around. I would remain vigilant, even if it meant expunging literature from my mind.

Disconcerted, my housemates continued to share their dream of a social life at the Annex. I merely decided to have another Coke.

Chapter 5

Madame Mumu and Morel were determined to spend some time together in the kitchen. They would get to know each other, talk of this and that, quickly forgetting my disturbing comments. Mumu would tell Morel about the misery of recent months, her bitter setbacks and piercing disappointments, flouting the strict instructions to say nothing about our pasts. Being craftier, Charles would invent for her a moving story about his life and tribulations. He would make her laugh and cry, would awaken her pity and her flirtatiousness. Old man Turgenev had already rejoined them in the kitchen to strengthen the little group's bonds … With one of those handkerchiefs embroidered with his initials, as they once were made, he wiped away the sweat beading up on his forehead. The heat in the kitchen was making him uncomfortable. He was breathing noisily. He seemed happy, however, to meet such a charming young man. As ambassador or vice consul assigned to Germany or Slovakia, he would be less demonstrative with him than his wife, but he would become just as convinced of the exceptional value of Charles, their new ally. The Turgenev couple would mourn the absence of meals in their room or in the dining room. Like a pair of lackeys, they would be content with sandwiches, counters, and stools. At the very least at noon, for lunch. This sort of degrading arrangement was part of the deprivation and decline in which the ungrateful State made those that sacrificed themselves for it live. But then this boy definitely seemed extraordinary. What adventures he'd had, what culture he'd acquired, and what luck that a Frenchman was here … There were certainly people much more disagreeable and antagonistic than this mild-mannered young man. He came from a good and very wealthy family. He'd already shown in the way he cut the sandwiches that he seemed to be a marvelous companion in misfortune. Given the regrettable and deplorable circumstances in which they found themselves and the heat that was afflicting them, the Turgenevs couldn't be picky. This boy would remain a gift from the heavens; he would stand in as an unexpected son for their twilight years in captivity.

The role of an old couple's adopted and beloved daughter was not unfamiliar to me. Two years earlier, I had entered the life of the Fosters, Mary and Brian. I had enchanted them, and then one day, fairly recently, just before my exfiltration, I had shot both of them in the head. And yet my friendship with these people had seemed real. I had developed a deep affection for them, knowing all the while that I would surely have to eliminate them. Which I did without blinking an eye. Something in me could see myself in this young, hypocritical flatterer who had, perhaps, truly become friends with the Turgenevs.

Nevertheless, *Teorema*, about whom Pasolini had made a fabulous film, briefly came to mind. I needed a more cultural reference than my own life. I couldn't bear for long the comparison of my character with that of the young Frenchman. So I allowed him a moment as a stand-in for Terence Stamp. I imagined the possibilities accordingly. Would he end up sleeping with the Annex's residents? Was he preparing to charm us? He claimed to have Celestino in his pocket and now the Turgenevs as well. How did he plan to deal with me? Had he already decided that his hostility toward me would be the best way to reign over his court?

I quickly abandoned the reference to *Teorema*. It was useless because it kept me from getting a good read on the capricious young man who had come into the kitchen, throwing a tantrum and playing the diva. Charles Morel was still a more plausible character for this kind of guy: cunning but cowardly. He was nothing like the Visitor, Pasolini's destructive messiah portrayed by the extraordinary Stamp in the film version of the work. He remained a schemer, a mediocre creature with no power to change the people around him. I wouldn't hesitate to shoot him dead if I felt the need.

I had scarcely left the room and already the Annex housemates were heaving a sigh of relief. As they saw it—and as I could tell from their forced smiles—the vile and vulgar woman was finally leaving ... Good riddance ... They'd have to isolate that one and take action to turn future new arrivals against her, especially the president's ex-wife who would be arriving shortly. She seemed to be a charming lady, capable of seducing the big-wigs of this world whom she had "dated" for a quite some time, as had been documented in the media. I wondered for a moment what ruse Morel was going to employ to beguile the star but, determined to explore the premises where I was held prisoner, I removed myself from the kitchen.

Upon entering the hallway, I saw two eyes staring at me from a distance. It was clearly the Cheshire Cat that I'd noticed a little earlier, before the meal, lying on a chest of drawers. It was waiting for me under a chair to guide me through my tour of the premises. This cat had surely been here, haunting the residence for years, or perhaps had—like the life's castaways that the Turgenevs, Morel, and I were—just settled in, hoping to find the *Raft of the Medusa*. Had the cat visited the apartment's previous residents whose fate I dared not guess? Or had it decided to move in the night before, seeing that this big apartment, empty for too long, was finally filling up with potential canned-kitty-food providers whom it would be easy to win over?

From afar, the cat suddenly beckoned. It came out of nowhere, from the shadows of a mysterious past, probably from the scorching hot alley of an unattainable Montreal. It bore the secret of its existence, which I would certainly never know, but it seemed to be here for me. In no time, I found a name for it: Moortje, like Anne Frank's cat. This cat wasn't Mouschi, the very gentle black cat that Peter, the van Pels' son, had been able to bring with him to the Annex and that Miep had taken into her home after all the occupants of 263 Prinsengracht had gone to their death. The Nazis had chosen not to send the cat to the camps. One might wonder why. Despite what is said, there was nothing rational about the extermination's logic, and cats could have been part of the final solution. Why not? I didn't think this cat bore any greater resemblance to Moffie, the guardian of the jam factory in which the Annex was cocooned. No, he didn't resemble the big black and white biscuit-thieving tomcat who had a tough time keeping the building free of rats and mice. The two eyes that appeared to me out of the dark belonged to Moortje, the cat that Anne had left behind when she left for the Annex one July morning. The cat that she said she constantly yearned for: "I miss Moortje every minute of every day, and no one knows how often I think of her; whenever I do, my eyes fill with tears. Moortje is so sweet, and I love her so much that I keep dreaming she'll come back to us." The animal under the chair a few feet away looked to me like the cat you'd have back home. It was the one whose death you cry about, the one that leaps from the darkness onto a bed on melancholy nights to solicit a caress, or even the one that never quite allows itself to be caught. It resists the desperate signs of affection offered by the fools who believe themselves to be its owners. It was the cat that leaves for five days or five months to live with the neighbours or in a park at the other end of the world, only to return and head straight to its bowl of water, as if nothing had happened and without deigning to raise its eyes toward the humans who welcome it back, touched to think that they hadn't been forgotten … It was the cat that gets left behind because he doesn't seem like the type to travel, the cat that you dream of seeing emerge from the dark to fall asleep purring on the next pillow. It was the cat that roamed the boarding school of my Swiss childhood, the one that came into our dormitory at night, meowing, and that disappeared during the day while we searched for it, calling, "Here, kitty, kitty!" Yes, this was Anne's Moortje, my cat, the one who said, "Look, I'm back, little one! I hope you weren't too worried while I was away. You even acted as if you could live without me. But now you know that isn't true. You need your cat to guide you toward your future … Everything will be fine."

I leaned toward Moortje, hoping to take him in my arms and make up for lost time. But Moortje looked at me in outrage. How could I assume that I was the one who made decisions about his life? Without further hesitation, he left at a run only to stop, like a king, in the middle of the hall. He wanted me to follow at a distance. Like a real cat. Caught off guard, I docilely submitted to his tacit commands. I went with him, following in his little footsteps, which oddly made the floors creak.

His hindquarters, which I saw moving down the hallway, led me first to a small room that must have once been the maid's, located back in a corner right next to the kitchen. The unmade bed and towels on the wood floor were indications that this was Morel's room. There was a minuscule bathroom to its right. This is where Charles had, because of me, taken his cold shower. At the window of this cramped room, a miniature fan stirred the humid air and struggled to create a breeze … The cat sat his rear end down on the still-damp towels for a moment, perhaps to cool off, but since I turned back toward the hallway, not wanting to linger in Charles' room, he gave up the comfort of the moist fabric and wove through my legs to urge me forward. He was orchestrating my visit.

I went back to the living and dining rooms. I realized then what I hadn't noticed before the meal: the rooms, even those that

I thought were at the front of the apartment, opened onto inner courtyards. They offered no view of Montreal. The apartment had been designed or remodeled like a labyrinth. Its opening onto the world consisted of nothing but a series of gloomy little garden plots. We'd have to get used to fixing our gaze on the more personal, private things we had.

Moortje didn't stay long in the big rooms, while my attention was caught again by the considerable number of books they held and was briefly tempted to see if I could find the Turgenev works that Mumu and her husband had brought to mind. But the cat forced me to continue my inspection. Without hesitation, he led me behind the living room where there was a slightly hidden, rather low door that an average-sized person would have trouble passing through without crouching down. Since the cat began to meow in front of the door, I opened it, both curious and cautious. I most definitely still missed my pistol … And yet I had no reason to be concerned. The Annex was being monitored, and it seemed unlikely that a hostile agent was hiding there. Enemy commandos didn't pull any punches. They came in with submachine guns to take everyone down. In fact, my only enemies were currently chatting in the kitchen, busily looking for a leaf of lettuce and a pickle to stick in their delicious jailhouse sandwiches.

As soon as I opened the door, Moortje darted into the darkened stairwell. He left me alone in the obscurity I'd just revealed. I didn't move a muscle. I listened with a keen ear. No sound seemed to come from below. My eyes quickly grew accustomed to the lack of light. By feeling along the upper part of the wall to my right, I found the switch I was looking for.

A lightbulb on the ceiling lit a small hidden staircase leading to the floor just below the apartment. Not entirely trusting the passage to which Moortje had led me, I slowly descended twenty rather steep stairs only to discover another entryway, this one immense and equipped with two vermillion door panels, which I pulled toward me with only the slightest hesitation. For a brief moment, I saw myself as Lewis Carroll's Alice when she ends up in a room whose every exit was locked. With a sinking heart, she wonders how she'll get out. Just then, she finds the key to a tiny door opening onto a space no bigger than a mousehole. But my training in suspicion and defensive strategies prevented me from tumbling Alice-like into the fictional well … I didn't climb through to the other side of the mirror. A quite capricious cat, who was very much alive, was meowing in front of the door, demanding that I open it. I came to my senses.

I really had to stop thinking in terms of books. I owed it to myself to rid my mind of these associations with absurd notions that prevented me from seeing things clearly, that had made me live with fantasies since the morning. It was Celestino's fault. The man had cast a spell on me. I was sure of it.

I turned a handle. The big door opened easily onto an astonishing room with a very high ceiling. It almost matched the footprint of the apartment where I and the other inhabitants of the Annex were housed. The wood-panelled walls were very white. Three large, well-placed chandeliers lit the space. In a different era, this stairway tucked away between two doors may have served as a barrier, a border fence protecting some sort of illegal activity. But in Montreal, what might someone have needed to hide from? It could have been used as a clandestine bar or perhaps a ballroom. In what world had this novel-worthy room been designed, hidden as it was in this old apartment with viewless windows? Was I in a cellar in Chicago? During prohibition in the 1920s, a number of basements had indeed housed exclusive clubs where people could drink and party, believing they were safe from police raids. So where was I? In which American city? I had landed in New York after my stopover in Reykjavik, then I'd taken another plane, blindfolded and flanked by two no-nonsense guards. The flight had taken one or two hours, tops. I couldn't be anywhere but the United States or Canada, not far from the east coast or right on the shores of the Atlantic.

Without giving too much attention to the questions that sought to trouble my mind, I allowed myself a moment to be dazzled by this extraordinary room. In my Annex, I would never enjoy a lovely view of the city, but I would have access to a grand ballroom in which others had surely loved to dance. As for Anne Frank, when the employees had finished their day, she had nothing but factory offices, which couldn't compete with my basement. I searched the walls and flooring for signs of the room's previous use. In vain. Everything seemed brand new. The room seemed to have been remodeled so that the Annex's residents could either do their first dance steps or attend their last ball there. What was I to think about such a place? I could not give in to book-based connections, which were already jostling about and would fill in for the lack of signs to decipher. I didn't want to abandon the idea that the Annex and its basement were located in my grandparents' city and, since I was constantly thinking about literature, my associations led me to settle on the surprising character of Khinyakov from Leonid Andreyev's short story, which had just popped into my head.

The sickly Khinyakov had decided to move into a cellar with thieves and prostitutes. At night, he saw what the others didn't: an enormous ash-coloured body, shapeless and terrible, that moved slowly, an incarnation of his own death. Was I in Khinyakov's fictional cellar? At least Russian authors push us far from reality. With them, the lived experience proves to be too dreadful and serves only as a pretext for dreams or nightmares. But I decided not to try to search my early memories for the end of Andreyev's tale and Khinyakov's final moments before dying. I had no idea where that might lead me. I needed to stay in the present, and since Moortje had fled across the room and out of sight, I began to search for him.

The air seemed fresher. Without realizing it, I'd left the Annex's fetid clamminess, which had become almost familiar since my arrival. At first, I thought it was the humidity that cooled the basement, but I soon noticed that an air conditioner filled each of two small windows located at the back of the room, maintaining the immense chamber's pleasant temperature. Carpets laid here and there divided up the vast wood floor. I don't know why, but I took my sandals off and stepped onto the plush wool. I wanted to feel the ground beneath me, and my feet—slightly swollen by the heat—enjoyed this freedom.

This magnificent and unexpected place was right underneath the Annex. Was it really part of it? For whom had this ballroom, with its ceiling lights that danced in the cool air, been built? I was unwittingly taken back to my last mission, to the Fosters' splendid house where I'd lived off and on for two years. I chased away my past with a wave of the hand. Slowly, with my feet equally appreciating the carpet's tender comfort and the hospitable chill emanating from the wood, I walked the entire length of the room.

I kept an eye out for the cat. He wasn't there. I noticed another door at the back and to the left of the huge room, and when I reached it, I promptly pushed it open. Moortje had definitely disappeared, and I wondered for a fraction of a second, and not without a twinge of regret, if I had lost him forever.

I saw a small gymnasium filled with three gleaming machines and exercise equipment. Several mirrors covered the room's high partition walls. They almost endlessly reproduced the youthful figure of a man of my age who was running on one of the two treadmills. The gym had been designed so that people like me, or like the guy drenching his machine with sweat, could train without regretting too much their early morning jog on the mountain or in a park.

From a distance, the man seemed to be a normal person in an Annex like ours. He was one of those humans that you could easily picture in a safe house. He was nothing like the wacky characters in the kitchen. He was running. He was thinking of putting his time in captivity to good use. He still believed he needed his highly trained body, and the rest of his story would indeed prove him right. I thought with a smile that he could easily land the role of imprisoned spy in a thriller. There was something a little insipid and combative about him that fit well with this kind of character.

Still sprinting along the treadmill at a rapid pace, he briefly turned his head to size me up. He quickly ascertained that I was unarmed. The sandals held in my hand could not pose a real threat. A creature like me was still quite unremarkable. I was like him. A rather nondescript agent, who could look harmless to a lot of people. The Annex was not just a refuge for the crazies, traitors, and cowards I had met earlier. It accommodated normal, brave spies who had neither reckless courage nor notable characteristics. Civil servants, like me …

The runner gave me a friendly wave with his left hand, thereby indicating in an obvious and authoritarian way that conversations and explanations would be deferred until later. At the appropriate time and place … He had no intention of slowing his regular, confident pace. The silence we kept was a comfort to me. Of course, I couldn't resist dubbing him Meursault because I immediately saw him as a banal, insignificant man who was, more importantly, capable of the worst … Yes, he undoubtedly could have killed a man on the beach or failed to attend his mother's funeral. He'd have no regrets at the time of his own death and would perish, thinking only that the end may have come a tad too soon. He was therefore a Meursault. Just like me. A creature ready to commit evil acts, without giving it too much thought. And yet to him, I must have looked like the pitiful Emma Bovary, so vapid I might have seemed with my sandals in hand and my feet all swollen. Like Emma, there was nothing exceptional about me. I had been an excellent Agathos agent who'd recently made a mistake, as do so many people who nevertheless have a talent for the profession, and I was in the habit of vacationing in Amsterdam so that I could pay a visit to Anne Frank. I did in fact lead a very orderly life and lying dormant within me, as it did in Emma, was a bored girl overly influenced by her past reading.

I had once tried to understand the human species through reading. When I was young and studying literature and philosophy in the United States, Germany, and Russia, I used to invent lives for other people, during complicated exercises that were simultaneously intellectual and spiritual. My reading helped me decode tons of signals coming directly from the bodies, gestures, and actions of those around me. From them, I created the framework of a fabulous story that I could change at will. Later, on the job, this training had seemed useful. In the secret agent's profession, conjuring up the missing pieces of a story or a life is appropriate. It's about interpreting in order to make the right moves. For the spies working for Agathos or Echthros, and indeed for all human beings, it is important to come up with a coherent fabrication about oneself and about others. Within the framework of this invented world order, events are classified. They submit to a rationale (fictional of course, but how can that be avoided?) that leads to action.

Over the years, I'd had to abandon my endless novelistic speculations about other people. Wandering and daydreaming had been quite natural to me. Especially when I was living at the boarding school, far from my family. Over the course of my life, I've learned to abridge—to concoct short, precise narratives. I made quick decisions. I chose to run or to stay or even to draw my weapon. My ability to absorb clues, characteristics, and symptoms had to a certain extent disappeared. It had given way to a controlled state of observation, to a constant monitoring that would leave me with nothing but response strategies. From the marvellous openness to the thoughts of others that we have when we're young, time creates a psychological police state. No longer can just anyone enter our psyches. At least that's what I believed to be my rule of thumb for a very long time.

I was thrilled at the sight of the machines systematically placed around the room. In the days to come, I could get back in shape, leave behind the books and the lazy mornings that I'd allowed myself that very day without even realizing it … I was going to keep playing sports so that I wouldn't get sidetracked by my reading. Like my Meursault, the runner stubbornly maintaining his athletic physique, I would try hard to believe that this interlude at the Annex changed nothing, that exercise could still be useful for what was to come, for a future in which life would be as it was before. I had to lie to myself, or at a minimum, not think too much because my brain knew very well that an eventual departure from this place implied either death or a radical metamorphosis. If I were lucky enough to survive this captivity, I'd have earned a life in which I would appear to be a very different person, living in a dreary city or town under an assumed name.

Would I be able to visit Anne again sometime in the future? The Franks' house had become mine many years ago. But I was far from any sort of departure from the Annex. Anne's diary had revealed that despite all her hopes, she had come to a bad end. A violent death is what awaits unwilling shut-ins like us.

A cat rubbed its head against my legs. It walked on my feet … Now it had followed me into the gym and urged me not to linger in this part of the basement. Moortje was there, and I was overjoyed, although he'd been gone for only three minutes. The fear of losing this animal whom I had just barely met seemed foolish, but it had already taken hold. I'd become attached to the cat who'd come out of nowhere. He ran off toward the former ballroom or clubroom and quickly leapt across it. He turned back. We'd seen enough of it. I watched him go through the red doors and disappear into the Annex's stairwell. He climbed back up toward the bedrooms and the dining room. I decided to do the same and left Meursault to his absurd run toward the future.

As I retraced Moortje's path, I thought about a different cat, Micetto, the one that Pope Leo XII entrusted to René de Chateaubriand when he died. In *Memoirs from Beyond the Tomb*, Chateaubriand writes that he seeks "to make him forget his exile, the Sistine Chapel and the sunlight of that cupola of Michelangelo's over which he would prowl, far from the ground." I'd always thought it strange that a writer as perceptive as Chateaubriand is endowing the cat with nostalgia for his past. If pussycats are by definition exiles, they do not dream of any specific homeland, any place that might have been their own. They are at home wherever they go and "seem to fall into a sleep of endless dreams," as Baudelaire writes, dreams that cannot focus on a specific location. Chateaubriand had been wrong about the Pope's cat, who in fact missed nothing and no one. Nothing could be more obvious. Maupassant had understood this in his text on cats where, if I remember correctly, he writes about the freedom of the animal, which owns the world and which in old homes, enters and leaves through cat-doors, those endless narrow passageways in the walls that go from cellar to attic. Moortje didn't have anything left to forget either. He lived in the present in the Annex. He encouraged me to do the same.

I was going to go back up to the world above as well, perhaps to take a little nap during which I hoped Moortje would come stretch out at my feet. But he would decide to go wherever he pleased. He might even lie down alongside Morel or the Turgenevs, the little traitor. I shouldn't expect any loyalty from the cat. I felt tired. This new existence was making me weak, lazy, and a little melancholy.

I was climbing the stairs, having carefully closed the double doors that kept the fresh air in the basement, when I bumped up against the other door, the one at the top of the staircase. It was locked from the outside, from the upper floor of the Annex. Moortje had disappeared through some unknown egress. Just as I was preparing to go back downstairs to ask Meursault if this was a common occurrence and if by chance he had the keys, the light bulb that I'd turned on when I first went downstairs went out. Evidently, a different light switch, one outside the staircase, had just been used. I found myself in the dark. I considered descending the stairs more quickly to regain the light of the ballroom's magnificent chandeliers. Then, as I opened the double doors, I realized that Meursault was standing at the doorway, sweating profusely. Did he want to speak to me? He was the one who had, deliberately or not, turned off the light using the switch at the bottom of the stairs. Was he trying to scare me? To see what I was made of? He turned on the little bulb, which cast scant light on the steps. Without saying a word, he hurried past me, leaving me, perplexed, to climb back up behind him.

His body odour was strong and unpleasant, and I did not want to linger too long with him in that narrow space. He was already opening the upper door leading into the Annex with a little key that he'd taken from the pocket of his shorts. Before liberating us from our shared confinement, he turned to me and calmly said, "It seems that you were a good agent. In fact, I know you were an excellent recruit. But you made an error … *Da bist du ja! Erinnerst du dich nicht an mich?* We've already met. *Du hast vergessen …* You're a little careless. That weakness is what landed you here, am I right? It's better to forget these somewhat less than glorious moments. Be cautious, more meticulous. Remember your mistakes. *Lern aus deinen Fehlern.* For example: Don't let anyone trap you between two doors, pretty lady! Who here would wish you well? You must pay more attention, my dear Anna … Yes … Anna. And you haven't the faintest idea who I am. You're the type of agent who always thinks that it's less courageous to bomb a besieged city than it is to kill someone with an axe. That's your Dostoevskyesque view of the world. You always think you're right. Perhaps, perhaps. Never let yourself be caught between two doors, Anna. Someone could kill you. Don't trust anyone and certainly not our devoted hotelkeeper. One never knows … *Man weiss ja nie.*"

The door had just cracked opened enough to allow the light and Meursault's body to pass through it. Without a word, I fled down the Annex's winding corridors and returned to my room.

Chapter 6

Celestino dragged me from sleep when he abruptly opened the door. In a single day, he had adopted the habit of waking me by entering my room unannounced. I tried to pull the sheet up to cover my face so I could go back to sleep, but I had no such cloth at my disposal.

Due to the heat, I had again stretched out on the bed without pulling back the covers. I too was developing bad habits. Moortje, who had laid down at my feet earlier and had, like me, taken a little siesta, now beat a hasty retreat. Lola began to bark and run after the cat, who had slipped through Celestino's legs. It wasn't long before she came back to her master. A lazy thing, she wasn't about to chase Moortje around the Annex. Celestino threw onto my recumbent body the contents of the bags full of clothes he'd just bought for me. It was a rude awakening. Over a few colourful sweaters, he asked, "But what are you doing with that filthy creature … Kick him out … Am I waking you up, my Sleeping Beauty? I hope you had pleasant dreams! You're crazy to sleep with that furry fleabag. That one comes and goes as he pleases; I have no idea where he comes from! I would gladly sprinkle his food with poison if I wasn't afraid of killing my Lola, who eats anything left lying around. A real gourmand, and yet she keeps her hourglass figure. Like you … If that cat ever hurts Lola, I'll strangle him with my own two hands … Don't let him back into your room, I'm sure he has scabies … That thing is a scuzzy beast. And besides, Lola would be jealous. You're not going to cast her aside for a leprous cat that has surely contracted leukemia, or worse yet. He traipses around all over the place … You know that Proust wrote a letter to Zadig, Reynaldo Hahn's dog. In it, he wonders whether it's better to be like animals that lack intelligence, books, and plans, or to be a learned creature … Not an easy question to answer. Am I really smarter than my Lola? That little one leads me around by the nose. Have you noticed that there aren't many animals in *In Search of …*? I don't understand why not, although Aunt Léonie, you know, the one who's always in bed, like you today, looks out her window and watches all the mutts that come and go in Combray. She wants the list of owners she sees strolling around outside with their pooches. But Proust didn't have a cat or a dog … I don't want you to get attached to that disease-ridden thing … At least keep him off your bed …"

I tried in vain to rouse myself and convey to Celestino that his presence was disturbing me. He went on anyway.

"Well … Here's what I found, Albertine, so that you'll be the best belle of the ball. I spent too much time shopping for you. I didn't have time to buy your clothes on the Internet. I wanted everyone to have something a bit chic to wear to dinner tonight … You know how attentive Proust's Titine was to the cut of other people's garments. And when she's a prisoner like you, the narrator goes out from time to time to order outfits for her. He copies Madame de Guermantes's clothes. Do you remember? Today, I couldn't base my choices on anyone. I just guessed at what to buy for a skinny-Minnie like you … Look, it's better to be thin than fat … At least that's what I tell Lola … I hope you're not like Albertine, who covets the most expensive things precisely because she doesn't have the money to buy them for herself. Poverty feeds desire, as we learn from Proust. I didn't find you any Fortuny gowns. On the other hand … I thought long and hard about your wardrobe. With this heat, I had to rack my brain to rustle up something fresh and cool. I don't want you to have sweat rings under your arms. I noticed that you sweat a fair amount … Anyway, that's the way you are, you can't do anything about it. Use a stronger anti-perspirant that will block everything … The salesgirls found me insufferable … It would take more than that to make me leave. They're idiots who don't even take the time to help their customers … Young people these days … Anyway, for tonight, I suggest a fluttery little lilac top with a round collar that you can wear with this loose-fitting pair of celadon pants. And I bought you a few bracelets in a thrift shop for next to nothing. I know the lady who runs the store … Yes, I know the important people in Pittsburgh … And you thought you were in Montreal! Don't you find that it smells like Pennsylvania here, Andy Warhol and *tutti quanti*? Don't be a sourpuss, you know perfectly well that the king of Pop Art was born in Pittsburgh. Too bad you can't go out to see the museum dedicated to him … You don't believe me? You prefer your Canadian fantasy? Suit yourself! I also took the liberty of buying you some cosmetics. You'll see, the pink lipstick will suit you especially well, it will bring out your green, blue, brown, or violet eyes … Depending on what I want to see in you … Here, tonight, you will all be my creatures, and you in particular, my Albertine … You have eyes that change according to my stories about you. And now look, I even got you sandals. Not wooden ones either. You're no peasant woman. This morning, while I was tidying your room, I checked your size … You'll be beautiful for this dinner. Saturna is busy cooking, she had to throw the old folks out. They wouldn't leave the kitchen … Kings like playing the lackey … A little meat will fortify you. Don't tell me you're a vegetarian! I wouldn't believe you, and besides, that wouldn't change your meals in the least … Everyone is getting ready. This will be our first Last Supper together. A lovely gang of friends-to-be, wouldn't you say? And this evening, Madame de Sévigné will grace us with her presence along with her 'sister,' or so she says. Don't give me that wide-eyed stare, Albertine, you look like a dead fish. Put on some kohl, okay, so your eyes won't look so glassy … I should have bought you some drops, or even an eyewash. It looks like your lids are stuck to your eyeballs … Mata Hari, you know who that is, don't you? The one the newspapers and TV broadcasts have been talking about over the past few days. She escaped with her life. They weren't shy, and they tried to kill her in the street in front of everyone. She's all you see on TV, you can't say she travels terribly incognito, she has a personal bodyguard, a *female* bodyguard, I should've said, a big woman who'll stay posted outside her room in case one of my prisoners or I myself should be tempted to gun her down … The lady guard dog looks a killing machine, despite her age. Rumour has it that she worked for none other than Qaddafi. You remember … The Amazons, those beautiful, tall, voluptuous girls. It was said that the tyrant was protected only by young women. It wasn't true. They actually served as sex slaves that he offered to his henchmen. How is one to know? Perhaps you could discuss this with her, inquire discreetly, even if she doesn't seem receptive. In any case, the woman is of a certain age, but as gorgeous as a goddess or Dorian Gray … She must have had a ton of plastic surgery. Well, okay, that's another story. Mata Hari has turned up with her 18-year-old sister … a charming young lady. I'll bet that she's her daughter and not her sister, but you know, in this line of work, one can't announce the existence of an 18-year-old child. One must try to hide one's age … Do you remember your history of French literature? Your classics? Françoise Marguerite de Grignan found it difficult to live without her mother, Madame de Sévigné. And Madame de Sévigné without her daughter. They wrote each other beautiful letters. You know literature better than I do. I'm already calling the girl Marguerite, after the daughter of Marie de Rabutin-Chantal, who was in fact better known as Madame de Sévigné. They've just arrived … They're very friendly, despite the rumours circulating about the mother: They say that she was the

Russian president's wife, that she had access to everything for years, and all the while she was working for us … You can imagine how furious our enemies are. A story worthy of a bad whodunit … But get up, for God's sake! I'm nothing like the narrator with Mademoiselle Simonet! I will not be spending my evenings watching you sleep and claiming, 'I spent delightful evenings chatting and playing with Albertine, but never so sweet as when I was watching her sleep.' Rubbish! No, you snore, my girl, and I don't need your sleep to possess you completely. I'm a sorceress, and I hypnotize you … *I, Tituba, Black Witch of Salem* … You haven't read the book? You should … A great author, that Maryse Condé. I found you a blue coat, for the fall and even the winter. I know, I know … You won't be going out much at all … In fact, it's highly unlikely. But at least you'll have it. And one never knows, sometimes they transfer you to an igloo in Greenland. There's no Celestino there who thinks about your wardrobe. Pittsburgh is the northernmost hick town I've ever known. I would suffer endlessly if I were to lose you, you know … We don't know each other, but I already love you. Too much, perhaps. Yes, too much! You know how it is in our profession. It's better to avoid attachments. But for you, I would splurge. I was in a shopping frenzy. The Organization is paying. You all are still among the privileged … Do you remember when the narrator comes to find Titine, and she's wearing a nightgown? She hesitates between two coats to quickly cover herself up. He's decided to take her out; he wants to go to Versailles, and she follows him obediently, getting dressed in a flash. Then she puts on the blue coat, the famous blue coat about which *In Search of* … commentators have likely written many pages. I myself searched all of Pittsburgh to find you the blue coat. Not so easy! The boutiques in Paris and Venice are far away, and it was blazing hot on the street … Of course, we won't be going to Versailles this fall. We won't even be going outside, but I would like to find you Albertine's blue coat, the one that reminded the narrator of a radiant sky. Wouldn't you like that? I'm going to rustle one up for you, my little plucked ducky … I'll have time once you're all settled into the Hotel Budapest … Things will take care of themselves, at least I believe they will; in any case, I won't be poking my nose into everything quite so much. We have all eternity before us, you and I! You shall have your coat! Tell me, Titine, are you listening to me? Don't pretend to be asleep. I must go finish arranging the table; Saturna doesn't have very good taste. She's like Proust's Françoise, an exceptional cook when she wants to be … Let's just hope that's what she wanted today … Because sometimes I find her food truly disgusting. I see your face; you were thinking about Benito Pérez Galdós. Yes, maybe I thought of him too, with Saturna, but as it turns out, that's her real name. Or maybe not, but I don't remember any more. It was hot in the kitchen, and our Saturna had to throw the oldsters out, as I already told you … You've met them, of course! Let me guess … You thought of Balzac's *Collection of Antiquities* and the tight inner circle that the Marquis d'Esgrignon ruled over in his little country town … No? … So it's a no … wait, tell me which book you thought of when you saw them?"

I'd been silent since Celestino's boisterous entry. Before falling asleep, overcome by the heat and with Moortje at my feet, I'd promised myself to be wary of him. Meursault, the spy who apparently knew things, had cautioned me. But even without the warnings from the guy, who couldn't be trusted anyway, I'd understood that the master of our house was a danger to me. I had to treat him like a superb manipulator of souls.

With his Proustian discourse and his incessant chatter, Celestino presented a trap into which I could not help but fall. He suspected that I would ultimately give in to him. Very quickly, I too saw that I couldn't resist conversing with him. I didn't have the strength to be modest, even though I'd decided before my nap to stop thinking in literary terms: I had to win the game of references and quotations. In another life, I had devoted my life to the written word, and though I don't know why, I was proud to be erudite. I raised my drowsy body, propped myself up on my elbows, and looked Celestino in the eye. After a time during which my host was gracious enough to remain silent and wait for me to speak, I revealed—quite grandiloquently—that I had nicknamed the old couple "the Turgenevs." I noticed that Celestino seemed very attentive to the Russian author's surname, so I continued. "You know *Mumu* or even *Two Landowners*. With those two, that's the Russia we're dealing with. They're writing us a Turgenev short story or two, right before our eyes ..." Celestino was thinking, that much was clear. His one good eye was darting about, revealing his great astonishment. He began to emit an appreciative whistle. "You're right, Titine ... The name is particularly apt. You are the worthy daughter of your papa Celestino. Into my arms, kiddo! You've scored at least two points. You're still very strong, despite the jet lag! I'd also thought of Elizabeth Gaskell and one of her novels, or maybe a short story, but I must confess: I really had nothing suitable to show you. Bravo to you, then! I bet you studied Russian literature in a different life. You spoke to the old couple in their language. Touché, eh? I'm spying on you, but I can't take any credit. They told me earlier, when I went into their room. They were, shall we say, amazed by your Russian, even though they, as I'm sure you know, immediately hated you ... You don't attract the friendship of aristocrats, with your somewhat pretentious nature. A sort of Lucy Honeychurch in the E.M. Forster book ... You don't want a view of the Arno? *A Room with a View*. But you won't have that here; as you've guessed, we don't see much through our windows, Lucy. That's the way it is. You'd pass for a stuck-up little mademoiselle ... Doubtless, you are one ... Bravo, Turgenev, he's the author that suits them … I admit I wouldn't have thought of him. I'm going to reread *Mumu* tonight, at home, to better appreciate your idea … Tonight or tomorrow because after the meal, which may run long, I'll have to clean up. It will be a lovely party for you! Yes, definitely! A bit like Flaubert's agricultural fairs. The great writer was afraid he wouldn't be able to have all his characters converse with each other. He wanted that chapter to be like a symphony … I feel like Flaubert today; I'm going to bring you all together and feed you your lines. If I had time, I'd distribute scripts, but I'll be terribly busy until tonight. I'm going to have to make do with your vapidities. The president's whore, that great lady, is gracing us with her presence. We must definitely celebrate her attendance. She'll be there, with her daughter-sister and her bodyguard, as will the two old folk. Wait, I'm thinking about it. You all speak Russian. I do too, by the way, so I have to avoid putting us all next to each other. Have to combat the ghetto effect … Yes, I do speak Russian … You know that in Cuba, I couldn't avoid it. And then I'll have to make room for the French boy whom I adore, he's my kind of gigolo. Well, I admit it. He has the soul of a traitor … ready to do anything to succeed. Just the way I like them. My guess is that you couldn't help seeing Morel in him … He also complained about you, obviously! You see how well I know you … Are you enjoying these literary gymnastics? I knew it. It wasn't hard to guess. At this point, however, I'd take away a point because frankly, Morel seems too obvious, although of course the idea can't be anything but incredibly accurate. Yes, Morel and I in Charlus… no? Crazy in love with a young man who is somewhat foolish yet also capable of killing him. Minus another point. This isn't worthy of you, this simplistic thinking … we're not quite there, but who knows, by Christmas, when we can no longer stand to live all together any more and once he'll have disappointed me, the little darling, I will certainly threaten him …

The winters are long in the northern United States, and Pittsburgh is not immune to the cold, bleak season! I prefer to see myself as a Proustian narrator, you see, rather than as Charlus. I'm your jailer. And one day, you'll leave without letting me know. Saturna will be the one to tell me, the way Françoise told Marcel about Albertine's departure. But until then, in the evening, we'll play checkers together, we'll read, or perhaps play music. I, the homosexual, will quickly begin to worry about the company you keep, skinny girl that you are. I'll frown at every word that falls from your delicious little mouth when you speak to anyone other than me. I'll picture you sleeping with Gaddafi's Amazon. You'll drive me crazy or you'll arouse me. I will never know if I truly love you, or if I care about you because you could elude me and be with someone other than me. But here, in our living situation, chances are that very soon I will fully possess you, without ever fearing that you'll run away. You'll lose your charm and your appeal because I'll know everything about you. You'll often bore me, but at other times, I'll be mad with joy at the sight of you … Crazy! Once again, you'll notice how well I know my Proust. Since this morning, I've been struggling. I've been trying to remember *The Prisoner*, which is not my favourite book, far from it, but whatever it takes to please you, my Titine … So I'll be able to rediscover my love for you, whenever you speak to the young Frenchman or to the guy who's your own age, the one who spent the day working out. You must have met him, your Tarzan? A tad banal, but not bad … He's definitely going to try to seduce you. He is, however, much too old for me. I like only very young boys … Look, there's a bit of Arthur Cravan in him, don't you think … You don't get who it is? No, there you go again with that blank stare … You don't know anything about literature after all! Arthur Cravan, the poet boxer, who was over two metres tall? He was Oscar Wilde's nephew … Never mind. But you know, we have to leave the Russians behind, it's a bit limiting as far as literary knowledge goes. You'll tell me what you've named him. It was easy for me. I thought of Tarzan, even if I was ashamed of how little effort I put into it. And then later, of Arthur Cravan, who isn't a character, he's a writer, but we wont quibble … It didn't end well for him, by the way, he disappeared. His big body was never found, even though it would have been hard to hide …"

"You think I'm more of a Charlus than a narrator." So said Celestino, who wanted to appear a bit concerned about my opinion of him, even though he and I knew that it was only a pretense, a game he was playing. "I'm always changing my mind. So for this evening, I established the guest list, just as Charlus did at the Verdurins in *The Prisoner*. It really wasn't complicated: The entire apartment is invited to my meal. Madame de Sévigné thinks she'll be the centre of attention at the gathering, just as Madame Verdurin may have believed, but no, she will very quickly understand that I will steal her thunder and that tonight, I will essentially be putting her in her place. I'm the Government's harlot, not her. She gets more publicity than I do, of course, but I'm still a better prostitute than she is … You can imagine … I wouldn't be here to do your shopping if I didn't believe I was ready to play the whore. It's not just anyone who can become manager of the Hotel Budapest … This will be her introduction as Madame de Sévigné, the one the narrator's grandmother loved so much … She'll play only a supporting role in our little impromptu."

Celestino was talking as he put my new clothes on hangers. He took care to quickly show them to me as he picked each piece up off the bed.

These clothes did not represent the woman I'd become many years ago. Because of my work for the secret service, I'd almost always wanted to go unnoticed. For a long time, I chose clothes that revealed nothing about me beyond my anonymity. I didn't want to linger over the things Celestino had just bought for me and arranged in my closet. They reminded me of something within me that had been extinguished. In another life, the one I'd left, I might have chosen these very pants, this blouse, or this dress that Celestino wanted me to try on. They signaled a taste or even a truth in me that I'd tried to erase. How could Celestino have known so well the woman I had been? What file on me had he read? How was he able to awaken in me the little Anna, the one who'd died more than 20 years ago? And how could his predominance over me make me believe that he was speaking to the young girl I'd once been? Was Celestino inventing a past for me, without even discussing it with me, a past I'd been foolish enough to accept of my own volition? And Meursault, who knew my real first name, was he in league with Celestino? What interest did those two have in making me such an anachronism?

I was surprised to find myself thinking once again of *Kiss of the Spider Woman*, which had come to mind that morning as I listened to Celestino. As I recalled, the Argentinian novel presented a pair of prisoners, Luis Molina and Valentín Arregui, who shared a single cell for a few weeks. These two men, jailed in a Buenos Aires prison, had nothing in common. Molina had been incarcerated for a vague question of immorality, but in reality for his homosexuality or his cross-dressing and his relationships with minors. Valentín was a political prisoner, serious, scholarly, and a member of a revolutionary group that wanted to overthrow the government. I remember thinking, as I read Puig, of Jean Genet and his novel, *Our Lady of the Flowers*. Back then, novels seemed to carry on a dialogue, to address each other. I'd enjoyed imagining how hard the two captives tried to forget their life in prison, and I couldn't help but think that Genet, whom I had greatly appreciated, also transformed the places of confinement. He made a prison into a paradise or a brothel … Puig had turned a prison cell into a movie theatre. Molina thus spent his evenings telling Valentin about the movies from the 1940s that he'd seen when he was younger. Thanks to the screens that Molina conjured, both men managed to escape their dreadful living conditions.

Yes, there were certainly numerous similarities between Puig's two characters and the bizarre couple that Celestino and I were already forming. Without realizing it, I was beginning to get jealous of the intimacy that my jailer might be sharing with the other occupants of the Annex. I had just met my own narrator this morning, and I was already concerned that he was getting too chummy with all the residents of our hideout … I too was able to transform myself into Marcel. I dreamt of locking Celestino up and keeping him for myself … Could he be my prisoner, even though I was his captive?

I also had a few memories of the American-Brazilian film that Hector Babenco had made based on Puig's novel. Like Molina, and William Hurt who played him, Celestino was an excellent raconteur. He was already bewitching me with his stories and, like Raul Julia's Valentin, I found myself caught in the nets of words that my comrade-in-confinement cast out to me. In Puig's version, Molina sometimes invented half the film, and sometimes he very accurately reported the scenes that he'd liked, but every night, he stopped the story at the precise moment when Valentin was enthralled. Thus he kept his friend in suspense … I understood that Celestino was crafting extraordinary adventures that might please me and that soon, he would play on my desire, my need to hear them. The description of Pittsburgh, which I nevertheless saw as pure invention, fascinated me. His rereading of Proust, which he had been depicting since we first met, enchanted me. On second thought, there was something of Scheherazade in Molina, and in Celestino as well. Their storytelling craft, their pacing, their pauses, their silences were nothing but effects calculated to please their public. Unfortunately, I lacked the power of Shahryar, the king of Persia, and instead I was condemned to be assassinated by my princess of *The Thousand and One Nights*, my Celestino.

I was a young student when I began reading Puig's novel, and as such, I might have believed that Molina was just a compulsive liar who wanted to seduce the overly naive Valentin. I clearly remember that at first, I'd thought that Molina was foolishly trying to have sex in his cell with a fellow prisoner. A gay guy charming a straight guy by describing schmaltzy movies. It was a predictable story. But the plot thickened. Molina was actually tasked with pumping Valentin for information about the political group. I'd watched him as he gradually penetrated Valentin's psyche all the better to betray him, to get him to talk. Valentin revealed things about his love life, and then about everything else. Molina metamorphosed into a queer Judas, an incarnation of the evil forces found in Manichean literature. And then, to my great surprise, Manuel Puig's story took a different turn. At that point, I admit, I'd been blown away by the writer's talent. Molina wasn't just a petty snitch. He fell in love with Valentin in spite of himself, and the narrative became impassioned. The no-exit proceedings took an unexpected turn.

With respect to my own imprisonment, it seemed obvious that Celestino could play a Molina. Were we not rewriting, by distorting it, an excellent novel? Were we capable only of copying Puig? And didn't we belong in a two-bit spy novel instead? Celestino's strength lay in the way he was making me believe that since my arrival, we'd been in Proust or in Turgenev, if that's what I really wanted … And why not in Puig, even if he hadn't yet mentioned the Argentinian writer? The homosexual had often—too often—played the role of the traitor or the bad guy in movies. Would we avoid this hoary old chestnut?

Unnerved by the thought that Celestino was making me recite dialogues that he had reworked as he saw fit and that I subconsciously knew by heart, I kept quiet. I didn't mention Puig's story, even though this very appropriate reference would have given me a great deal of prestige in his eyes. Something within me refused to show him that I knew his plan. In any case, I was already losing my host's game. Literature had come back into my life. I was undoubtedly going to end up revealing all my secrets, as had Valentin. Had it come time for me to capitulate? What interest could this phony Cuban have in making me come clean?

"I brought you two peignoirs. I could have given them to Madame de Sévigné, who must be accustomed to silk, the hussy. As for you, you obviously don't wear fine fabrics every day, but here, with the heat, you'll appreciate the consideration. Like Madame Swann, you'll wear a light-coloured, crêpe de Chine peignoir. Tonight, you could wear a bouquet of violets on your blouse, if only I'd found those adorable little flowers. But in Pittsburgh in the middle of the summer, you'll find only daisies and a few wilted roses … This city's not known for its refined taste! For that, no! Are you listening to me, Albertine? You look like you're thinking about all the people you killed during your too-short career and all the men and women that are safe because of your imprisonment. Here, there's only me, the narrator, that you truly put to death by making him crazy about you."

Celestino went on, commenting on the outfits that he'd bought for me and, while I found these descriptions delightful, the comment about the executions I'd carried out within the very specific framework of my job had left me a little confused.

Why was Celestino so determined to remind me of what I'd done? What exactly did he know? I was in the Annex because I too had betrayed people very close to me. Neither Agathos nor Celestino was unaware of it. So why bring up the obvious? I'd recently been forced to leave too much of a trail. During my last mission, I'd killed two enemy agents who'd believed in my role as confidant. Each one had received a bullet in the brain, just when they least expected it. They were about to find out that I was a double agent, so I'd had no choice. I'd shot them while we were all sharing a meal that they'd prepared for my birthday … After blowing out the candles, I'd quickly executed them, before they'd had a chance to comprehend. And that's how good a friend I'd been! And yet I couldn't panic over this terrible act of betrayal. I had nothing to confess, nothing to regret. I had done my job. Not very well, incidentally. Because of my negligence, three other people had been flagged by Echthros. Now they were in a morgue or in a different Annex. Everyone could understand it. Celestino had nothing to squeeze out of me. I myself could not forget that I had exploited Mary and Brian Foster's trust. For two years, I'd played at being their adopted daughter, their protégé, and in one sense, I had truly been a good child. For two years, they'd had the most loyal friend, the most loveable family member. They didn't know it, but thanks to me, in their big luxurious house, they had escaped death. I had watched over them for 24 months so that they would share major secrets with me. They had done so. I had killed them according to plan. I had killed them at the appropriate time, after having kept them alive. If I hadn't eliminated them, they would have had me disappear … Had they harboured doubts about me? Had they come to mistrust me? To gain their confidence, I'd had to give them some compromising information, documents that in the end, I couldn't get back. That's what tripped me up! That's why I was in the Annex, with people who were surely false friends and on a mission to kill me. If I had reasons to blame myself, it was because I had exposed agents from the Organization. Having eliminated enemies was nothing serious in my opinion. Was I supposed to feel guilty?

Many historians have gotten lost in conjectures about the identity of those who denounced the members of the 263 Prinsengracht Annex. The people who had helped the Franks for over two years surely had little or no interest in revealing their own complicity. Nevertheless, an anonymous call made during the stifling summer of 1944 had led the Dutch authorities and the Gestapo to the Annex and the Franks to their death. According to Austrian author Melissa Muller, the woman who cleaned the warehouse in which the Annex was hidden might have delivered up the Franks, the van Pels, and Pfeffer. She may have been afraid that she and her husband would be deported for having been found guilty of aiding and abetting. Having lost a son in the war, she might have hoped to protect her husband and taken action. In fact, it's quite clear that the Franks had been betrayed by someone who had initially protected them. Although I saw myself as an Anne Frank in my Annex, I knew that I was still capable of playing the traitor's role. I'd always told myself that for Jesus to die innocent, he'd needed Judas. And I'd been a Judas, without even feeling bad about it. But the man or woman who betrays can also do so out of love for Christ … With Celestino, I was perhaps able to remain innocent. Could he become my Judas? Had I decided that he was going to deceive me? Why was I able to see myself falling into his trap while throughout my entire life, I'd violated the trust of others the better to destroy them? What were any of us—the Franks' informers and I, the Fosters' assassin—capable of?

"Ah! I forgot!" Celestino exclaimed as he pulled me from the confused reverie of my treachery. "I brought you some pretty little notebooks in which you could unburden yourself, or write your own *Diary of Anne Frank*. But I have so little hope … You're not the sort given to confessional writing … I see you as Sei Shōnagon. Scholar that you are, you must have read *The Pillow Book*, her collection of lists, poems, lamentations, anecdotes, reflections, and observations gathered during the time the author spent in Empress Teishi's court. In your case, you'll introduce the world to the Hotel Budapest and your master Celestino when you're published after your death, which will occur after many days of torture inflicted by the enemy. I will save your text for you, do not fear. For your posterity, my sweet!"

Celestino giggled as he put a packet of three bras in the linen closet. He took, however, a prophetic tone as if he were reading my future through my undergarments. "But as you surely have already guessed," he added as he collected the empty plastic bags, "it's definitely going to be me, and no one else, who will wring your last breath from you … In the meantime, be ready at 8 p.m. We'll all be there!"

Chapter 7

A large table had been set right in the middle of the ballroom and magnificently arranged to accommodate all the members of the Annex. Dressed like royalty thanks to the excellent care taken by our master of ceremonies, Celestino, they were standing around the vast room, glasses in hand. Despite the heat and fatigue, we hadn't dared defy our host's orders, and therefore none of us had taken the time to recover from the emotions aroused by the extraordinary circumstances that had brought each of us to the apartment. Celestino insisted on welcoming his guests. We were there, exhausted but ready to participate in the farce that our jailer had scripted.

The basement room where our meal was to be held was decorated ostentatiously. The three chandeliers had been turned off to create a more intimate atmosphere. Two large candelabras found who knows where presided over the tablecloth, giving the dinnerware an old aristocratic look. Near a tall white pedestal table sat bottles of a fresh little rosé wine, delicious in the summer, whose qualities Celestino was sure to rave about all evening. Such a décor could make us forget about our confinement and the danger threatening our existence in the Annex above. Celestino had decided that despite certain events, we deserved a little party. Nothing could thwart his plan.

I was reluctant to go over to the corner where everyone was getting to know each other. They were toasting to a new life whose uncertain nature they were forgetting. I had no desire to officially introduce myself to Celestino's guests, but I figured it would be difficult to avoid all these people when I was about to eat with them. I could probably steer clear of their embarrassing presence for the remainder of my captivity. Time was on my side …

In the first group, Mumu, Turgenev, and Morel chatted together as they stood around the pedestal table. Next to them, a little further back, an odd little man in his sixties sat slumped on a big worn-velvet loveseat installed for the occasion. Everything about him suggested a certain deformation that was accentuated by the twisted neck emerging from his starched white shirt, which Celestino must have given him to make him a little less frightening. I couldn't help but instantly compare him to Gregor Samsa, the character from Kafka's *Metamorphosis*. The man had awakened one day as a monstrous insect. His body had become a gruesome prison. His limbs had been transformed into legs. So then you need to imagine something even more horrific: the aging process, the accumulated years that had changed the figure and face of the handsome man he clearly once was into something grotesque.

It was he was who, having slowly risen from the sofa, promptly extended an awkward, gnarled hand. He urged me to have a glass of wine and very graciously introduced himself, telling me in a hoarse voice either his assumed or his real first name, Marcus, which he followed with a nervous, timid admission. He asked me to excuse the sweat rings that adorned his stiff white shirt. It was too hot for him and his body was very sensitive to the heat wave. I could tell. I smiled at him with feigned solicitude. When earlier Celestino had told me a little about each member of the Annex, he hadn't mentioned the existence of this strange bird. He evidently played an insignificant role in the bizarre novel that Celestino was writing.

I took advantage of Gregor Samsa's revelation to sit next to him under the air conditioner that cooled the room. I introduced myself to him, using the name Albertine.

Gregor chattered on. I listened to him. He was somewhat out of sorts. He was feeling very jet-lagged and wondered if he'd have the strength to spend the evening eating and acting cheerful, when he was taciturn by nature. He began to talk about his education in the sciences, his life as a physician, and his entry into Agathos at the age of 40, and to share his existential uncertainties. Never could he have imagined that he'd end up at the Hotel Budapest or in a safe house with this somewhat boisterous, overly ostentatious Celestino. No, never could he have imagined an end such as this.

I didn't reply. I didn't want to discuss the past or even nebulous possibilities. Gregor took notice, laughed, and quickly apologized for having revealed such things to me. He knew that he wasn't supposed to talk about himself and didn't understand why he was already telling me about his life, when he was doing all he could to remain silent. It was the jet lag that was making him capable of such excesses.

I thought that Samsa was right. It would have been better indeed if he hadn't disclosed his regrets to me. And Celestino should have waited before giving this banquet. Things were moving too fast. All it took was a glance around the room to see that we all seemed dazed with fatigue and ready to ease our suffering and incredulity by revealing the most compromising secrets or by openly giving in to despair!

Anne Frank herself doesn't describe in detail the first meal after the three van Daans—Hermann, Petronella, and their son Peter—came to the Annex, but she confides in her diary that the first day when the two families were together, they were all in a good mood when they ate. All the members of the Annex felt then that they were part of the same clan. We quickly learn how greatly the disputes and quarrels among all the Prinsengracht prisoners would unravel this blissful and instantaneous feeling of belonging. Did Celestino want us to avoid future conflicts by making this first party so pleasant? Or was he instead making sure that we all hated each other, forced as we were to suddenly make small talk?

I'd had happy moments during gatherings held by my hosts, the Fosters. These parties still haunted me; I'd learned to have fun there, despite the circumstances and my intentions. Just as Benjamin Guggenheim had done on the Titanic while the unsinkable ship was descending into the frigid waters and he knew he'd soon be dead, I had donned my most beautiful clothes and could announce to everyone present on Celestino's lifeboat, "We've dressed up in our best and are prepared to go down like gentlemen."

Standing near a chimney as he chatted with the second group of guests gathered around a seductive Meursault, Celestino surveyed the room. Like an orchestra's imperious conductor, he decided when we would enter the scene and when we would speak. I was hoping to play the part of second violin and allow the evening to carry me along by occasionally humming a familiar tune, with a "naturally" or an "oh yes" or a "how right you are" as my only reply to questions asked … I would idly try to understand the role that Meursault had played in my life, but his warnings didn't seem terribly shrewd. I had nothing to learn from him. I was a little concerned that I didn't recognize anything in the visage that Meursault was showing me. Against all expectations, literature was returning to me intact from the depths of time. So why had I forgotten this ordinary spy's face?

Celestino smiled at me from a distance. He appreciated the effort I seemed to be making to amuse myself. He was encouraging me. Lola was under his left arm, and he was forced to shift his weight from one leg to the other so that he wouldn't lose his balance when the dog, agitated by the evening's excitement, tried to move. What was this meal all about? What did he have in mind? I was tired; my mind was wandering. Was there something of Félix Krull, Thomas Mann's social-climbing impostor, in Celestino, or even of the Devil himself, as we see him in the guise of Woland in Bulgakov's *The Master and Margarita*? I wish I could have shut down the literary mechanism within me. The urge to give in to the pleasure of a delightful social event finally prevailed.

Morel gave me a little nod of the head that was both friendly and hostile, which I and Madame Turgenev, who continued to laugh with him, could each interpret in our own way. As for the Turgenevs, they greeted me with a forced "hello" in Russian, and then turned away to pursue their ongoing conversation with Charles. Envious, they were eyeballing the other group of Celestino's guests. Among them was Mata Hari, the media darling who appeared to interest them more than I did. I decided to sit with Gregor on the velvet loveseat, in an awkward attempt to join the party. We both observed Moortje walking across the hallway. Samsa quickly spoke to me: "I'd prefer to be like the cat tonight, to get out of here and stroll around the apartment, which I find quite lovely. Don't you agree?" Samsa asked in impeccable English. He had clearly spent part of his life in Great Britain or at least knew how to play the Brit to a tee, although I detected something of the Slav in him. Lola had also seen Moortje. She began a faint woofing. Like Samsa, she'd reconciled herself to this wasted evening.

I watched the guests as I sipped my second glass of rosé. Hunger was gnawing at me. Were we going to sit down to eat soon and be done with this sham of a cocktail hour or was I going to end up getting drunk in spite of myself, on a detestable overly sweet wine? From time to time, Meursault gave me a wink that no one else noticed. Although I couldn't remember what role he'd played in my past, I managed to see a large part of his soul. And I saw nothing worthwhile there. I tried to distract myself by soaking up the charm, the wine, the atmosphere, and the beautiful clothes.

Madame de Sévigné seemed to be living up to her reputation. She radiated an undeniable beauty. Her full round figure moulded into a black dress, she cheerfully conversed with her new friends.

Here again, Celestino had played the narrator, the designer of souls, and had given her a garment that conformed to her life as a high-class prostitute. But since she wasn't wearing any jewellery, her attire—though it highlighted her shapes admirably—gave her a somewhat bereaved look. Behind her stood Madame de Grignan, her sister or daughter, in a plain red pantsuit. This young woman of about 20 obviously had no idea what she was doing in the Annex. She kept her eyes on their bodyguard, Qaddafi's Amazon, as Celestino had dubbed her. This immense, grim-looking woman was busy calculating the threat level of each person. I immediately nicknamed her Dors Venabili as an homage to the robot protecting Hari Seldon, drawn straight from Isaac Asimov's imagination. She was wearing a black shirt-dress that suited her massive silhouette. A revolver in her waistband gave proof of her duties, which she never forgot. Yet there was something totally ridiculous about this display of protectiveness. She wouldn't last long if a commando unit armed with machine guns burst in on our party and decided to riddle our bodies with bullets …

It was on the basis of these highly practical considerations that I had left my pistol in my room. The people who wanted to kill me had planned their move well: They'd easily overpower an agent armed with a Sig Sauer in the deathtrap that was the Annex. Here, with my weapon, I'd be entitled only to suicide or assassination as one of the hideout's has-beens. I had lost all power to act. The lilac and celadon shades of my outfit were meant to make me look like an old maid. Why had Celestino costumed me as an apathetic, inadequate sylph? Although Albertine Simonet proved to be a dull creature on occasion, the narrator maintained that she had a rebellious, assertive temperament, and did only what she wanted to do. She had no respect at all for high society. Did Celestino recognize my contempt for all these mediocre double agents, these small-time spies like the Turgenevs, Morel, Gregor Samsa or even the group pathetically protected by Qaddafi's bodyguard? Why had he decked me out in such diaphanous clothes, and more importantly, why had I agreed to wear them? Had I truly become Celestino's prisoner?

Sévigné continued to chitchat in a calm, strong voice with Meursault, whose suit displayed his James Bond good looks and physique. She came up with a witty remark in Russian when the Turgenevs introduced themselves to her, making everyone laugh except Meursault and Morel. The two knew nothing of the language of Tolstoy and could only understand if conversations were conducted in English.

Old Mr. Turgenev wore a somewhat shabby smoking jacket with sleeves that were too long. Celestino had poorly estimated his size, and he hadn't even taken the trouble to alter the voluminous garment. Why hadn't Mumu taken action and hemmed her husband's jacket? She must have been exhausted by the past few days and the afternoon's chats with Morel. She'd forgotten about her husband's outfit! Despite the heat, she was sporting a little pink suit à la Jackie Kennedy in Dallas. But of course the ensemble was a failure. Mumu was too pale-skinned to wear this candy-coloured shade, which gave her a waxy appearance. I was ultimately convinced that Celestino had deliberately dressed the Turgenevs in frumpy clothes. The Cuban was lying to me about everything. He couldn't have bought these second-hand clothes and the four-seasons wardrobe for eight people in a single afternoon. He had received our physical descriptions and measurements a few days earlier and had worked long and hard to create or to destroy us, however he saw fit. Was Celestino perverse enough to have dressed us all in elegant attire only to have enemy forces assassinate us right in the middle or at the end of the meal? Did he want to turn our deaths into a final work of art? What book had been the source of such an idea?

Sévigné saddened the Turgenevs when she told the old folks, who were insisting on rekindling her memories, that she had absolutely no memory of ever having met them at home, at the Belarusian embassy in Greece one evening when the President had paid them a visit. The Turgenevs had insisted in vain, describing in great detail the meeting and the stunning outfit Sévigné had worn, though she denied ever having gone to Athens with the President, claiming furthermore that she didn't even know him! The Belarusians must be confusing her with a different wife. The woman certainly had nerve! She displayed a breathtaking impudence … She could be seen standing next to the enemy president on television stations around the world and on all the newspapers' websites, from the *New York Times* to *Die Zeit*, including *El Universal* and *The Sentinel*, yet she claimed not to know who the Turgenevs were talking about! I finally felt a kind of respect for one of my fellow inmates: Sévigné knew how to keep her mouth shut and especially how to lie. She seemed quite capable of killing in cold blood in order to protect herself. What more could one ask? The memory of the Fosters' assassination by Agent Francesca Connors came to mind. Yes, the person I'd been for two years shared many character traits with the Sévigné woman. And the sight of friends lying in a pool of blood wouldn't have disturbed her any more than it had disturbed me, the sweet and charming Francesca, the devoted daughter.

Sévigné silenced the sheepish Turgenevs by uttering an excessively emphatic "Charmed, I'm sure" in response to Morel, who was already kissing her hand. He immediately fell under her spell. And soon, I guessed, he would drop the laughable Turgenevs.

Celestino had tried everything in his power to keep Madame de Sévigné from becoming the queen of the ball. But he felt obliged to calculate the magnitude of the charisma that the woman exuded. In fact, she was already assembling a court of admirers.

Saturna came into the ballroom with two trays of appetizing hors d'oeuvres. Celestino hurried over to her and grabbed them from her hands. He shouted, "Look what we made for you today, while you were relaxing or touring the apartment. I deny my guests nothing. You're at home here. I want you to feel that. To me, you are all, without exception, distinguished people, men and women of duty, no doubt about it. The Organization knows this and thanks you for it. I myself will be here for you in moments of grace as well as in times of despair. But the work stops here. You are here with me for your entertainment. And now you must taste these little marvels posthaste." And already he was extending the platters toward his guests' hands.

I stood up to grab two or three of the appetizers still on a tray that had just been placed on the pedestal table. I hoped that the bread and pâtés would relieve my hunger a bit. Saturna had gone back up to the kitchen. It would be some time before she came back downstairs, her arms laden with food. Samsa began speaking Russian with the group of Slavic women, and Meursault and Morel hurried over to each other, babbling inanities about the wine … The conversations took a decidedly boring turn. With feigned jauntiness, Celestino even tried to create a feeling of community by explaining what a puzzler his choice of menu had been. He was speaking English with a strong Hispanic accent, which suddenly seemed vaguely authentic. Everyone joined the discussion, sharing obvious thoughts about food and culinary tastes. Meursault brushed against me as he passed by. The others must have surely imagined that he had some interest in me. He took advantage of this farce to whisper a name, that of a friend from my Swiss boarding school, Hélène Samroy, which I had a hard time understanding and which—as I saw from the way he told me so that no one else could hear—was supposed to be of great value to me.

Hélène Samroy … Why was this old and insignificant college friendship, this schoolmate whom I hadn't seen in 30 years, remerging in the Annex's living room? I gave Meursault a quizzical look, but his silence told me not to pursue it. He didn't want Celestino to see me talking with him.

We finally sat down at the table. I had no thoughts for anything other than the food I'd been imagining since the evening had begun.

The dishes had been chosen with care; it was abundantly clear that Celestino had carte blanche when it came to the Annex's upkeep. He hadn't forgotten Charles Fourier's principles in the strange phalanx that we formed, so before the meal, he joyfully read an excerpt from the Societarian School's founder: "Pleasure's first stimulus is good food. If people are malnourished, they won't be able to enjoy their work. They must have plenty of good bread, good meat, good vegetables, good fruit, good milk products, and good wines; as well as different varieties of poultry and fish, etc." Celestino would starve us later when we had no other choice but to eat from his hand. He went on with some Fitzgerald to explain the inspiration for the first course: "On buffet tables, garnished with glistening hors-d'œuvres, spiced baked hams crowded against salads of Harlequin designs and pastry pigs and turkeys bewitched to a dark gold." Everyone applauded these grotesque preliminaries. But it's true that the food was magnificent and that the sight of it added to the deceptive happiness of being there, safe in the middle of the Annex, and still among the living.

Celestino had seated me to his left and had assigned Madame Turgenev the seat to his right. I found Meursault sitting next to me. He whispered banalities in my ear and encouraged me to offer something harmless in response. I also tried to avoid Celestino, who complimented himself endlessly, confiding in hushed tones how brilliant his selection of food and clothing for his guests were. There seemed to be no happier man than he. Perhaps he was going to put off having the entire Annex massacred by an armed commando … After all, he surely must be hoping to see us suffer … I tried chatting a bit with the young Grignan who, as she sat facing me, explained how she would continue her ballet training in the marvellous room where we were lucky enough to be dining. She had been taking classes at the Paris Opera. With tears in her eyes, she told her tablemates how much she was going to miss her life as a free young lady. Her voice cracked. She was imagining what the next few years would be like. With a wave, Sévigné ordered her to be quiet and made it clear that she was behaving like a spoiled child untouched by fear, anxiety, or deprivation. She shot back, saying "Well, soon enough, you'll go back to your ordinary existence. Just like we all will!" The movement of her head perfectly illustrated her insouciance. The Turgenevs tried to fully support Sévigné's point of view. She was right to be seeing things that way. The young one needn't worry, things changed so quickly. Mumu even leaned toward Grignan to console her with a few words of Russian. They quickly went on to talk of the beauty of the room in which you could host a ball or present a dance solo … Everyone agreed with her ideas about the room's use. People got excited about the organization of communal celebrations, the list of films that could be watched together, and the possibility of a movie-lovers' club, which would be easy to establish. Celestino reiterated how generous Agathos was. He could order whatever we wanted to see. The thought of a group of movie-goers managed to completely turn me off of this bunch. After years of solitude and silence, they were all throwing themselves into a chatty community that would give them a sense of family that had been extinguished in them out of necessity. What a letdown!

I gave up trying to talk with the other guests, so disinclined was I to share anything at all with these accidental spies. I contemplated Anne Frank, who had written: "During meals, I talk more to myself than to others." And the thought of the young girl did me a world of good.

Who had all these people been? Social climbers, profiteers, second-rate double agents shocked to find themselves here, when they should have been living the life of luxury led by the international secret agents on TV? Wasn't I myself getting attached to this Celestino, the first human who, since my entry into the secret service, seemed like he might be my equal, my brother? I had loved the Fosters … They had been perfectly wonderful to me, but never did I forget that I would undoubtedly be called upon to eliminate them. Never had I believed that I might form some sort of family with them. And yet these people had given me everything.

The meal proved to be, despite my irritation, delicious. And eventually the wine made me less suspicious.

Celestino left the table to help Saturna get the dessert of chocolate profiteroles, which he knew I liked … Meursault promptly jumped on the occasion. He asked so that no one else could hear, "Don't you recognize me? For a spy, Anna, you're not much of a physiognomist. The moment I saw you in the gym, I knew who you were. I must admit that I have the list of the apartment's occupants. But you haven't changed much. Look me in the eye … Is it coming back to you? Hélène Samroy … her kid brother. Switzerland … We met several times in Geneva, when you were spending time at her house. Your mother didn't come to visit you very often. You weren't going to Nice to be with her either. You spent your weekends with us. You were a young girl, and I was a little younger. Maybe you didn't notice me, but I was fascinated by you. Because of …" Worried, he stopped and began again only once he felt certain that neither Celestino nor the others could hear him. "I'm here to spy on our host … Duplicity, *wer weiss*? I just wanted to let you know. Be careful … Hélène died. Cancer. In her honour." And he raised his glass, pretending to toast to his sister's memory.

Had I thought of Hélène Samroy, I would have said that she had a family and maybe, just maybe a brother, but I don't really remember that … Had I often gone to the Samroys when I was a child? As far as I knew, two or three times. No more than that. Hélène had been a nice friend who'd taken pity on me, the little orphan girl I appeared to be. Meursault had his reasons for lying to me or for wanting to talk to me. I didn't care to find out what they were. The possibility that Celestino was a traitor was becoming obvious. I wanted to think about it later. So I turned my back to Meursault to chat with the rest of my dinner companions.

Despite my aversion to all the people who were there to share my prison, I ended up having a wonderful evening letting myself get swept up by the foolishness of a happy moment. The profiteroles served with crème Chantilly cheered me up, and when bottles of champagne were brought out to conclude the meal, I raised my glass to my future in the Annex.

Later, a few of us danced on the large hall's magnificent wood floor. I even began an impromptu waltz with Celestino that I finished in the arms of Dors Venabili. The last time I'd danced, it had been with Brian Foster on the thirtieth anniversary of his marriage to his wife, my friend Mary. I'd had fun that evening. And I had just recaptured a little of that joy. Why not?

I went to sleep almost happy, my stomach full, exhausted.

Life was as sweet as a summer night in Montreal.

Chapter 8

I learned of Turgenev's death late in the morning on September 1. I was in the large living room, scanning the shelves, looking for a book for the day or the week. I dithered over a rereading of *Crime and Punishment* and a deep dive into a novel by Sofi Oksanen, a young Finnish author whom Celestino had praised. He had decided, after having mentioned the writer's name several times, to buy me all her works translated into English from the bookshop in Pittsburgh where he claimed he got his books. Pittsburgh … the city he had conjured up to satisfy my desire to know where we were. He wouldn't back down. I'd have to get used to the idea: The Annex was in a neighbourhood of Pittsburgh, not far from the university. A very good university, he said, with excellent departments of literature specializing in Slavic studies. They gave lectures there that I would have loved if only I'd been able to go to them. Too bad, since it was only a five-minute walk away, and at the end of September, there would be a seminar on the works of Akhmatova, and he had guessed my interest in her. I knew perfectly well, however, that Celestino had repeatedly told the Turgenevs that we were living in a beautiful New York building in the heart of Brooklyn and that he had bragged to Morel about the beauty of the old art-deco building in Detroit that stood right next to the one that housed us. I had heard the three friends discussing the various versions that Celestino had told them, and to their great astonishment, they had noticed numerous inconsistencies in our host's statements. In their opinion, they had misunderstood … Celestino couldn't have lied about the Hotel Budapest's geographical location. They considered him to be the very epitome of honesty and kindness.

I, on the other hand, was hardly surprised by Celestino's deceptions. For two months, I'd been able to keep a mental list of the contradictions in his stories, though I still found them amusing. My suspicion was so great that I couldn't decide whether I should read Oksanen, as my jailer friend had so advised. I was afraid of loving the novels that he had described at length and then bought for me at Amazing Books in Pittsburgh, or so he claimed, in a show of infinite kindness toward me. He hoped that we could discuss what we read. He and I were the only occupants who truly loved literature. He'd been very disappointed to realize that my companions in confinement were in fact far less educated than their social position or their pretentiousness would lead one to believe. Agathos had promised him very special agents, as he said with a laugh, a group of erudite men and learned women, to be a credit to the site and to the superb library he had established there. But we were way off the mark! We were dealing with nothing but ignoramuses! Even Madame de Sévigné, who had actually earned a degree in philosophy in her youth, didn't enjoy reading. Celestino had suggested that she try a few classics, which she hadn't even bothered to open. She'd had the nerve to request magazines and tabloid newspapers for her daughter, who was hoping to see how famous she was … "You see, it's not exclusively stories about faggots that I enjoy, and I do like certain female writers, those fine women who write aren't always rubbish, I must admit. I adore Arundhati Roy … And Oksanen, I swear you'll like her," Celestino had told me joyfully.

There I was, trying to escape Celestino's obscure literary stratagem by finally trying to live with Raskolnikov for a few days, when Meursault entered the living room, slipped up beside me, pretending to look for a book, and whispered right next to my ear, "The old Russian man died during the night. They already took his body away. I woke up when he began to feel ill, sometime around midnight. I'd just fallen asleep. I heard the gentleman moan for a good hour, complaining about pain in his stomach. He was suffering, that's for sure. Saturna knocked on my door. She asked me to help her. She wanted to move him downstairs, so he wouldn't be so hot. We put him on a little makeshift mattress. Actually, all of us should be sleeping in the big hall or the gym … We'd have more air … He got some of his colour back. His wife was watching over him. Saturna went to make him a tisane and some rice water. I decided to go back to bed. Saturna had just informed our ridiculous master of ceremonies. Do not trust him, Anna, I won't stop telling you. And Saturna, who has only the official version, gave me the news of his death this morning. They didn't have time to send for the doctor. The old man apparently had terrible indigestion, and at his age, and with his known heart condition and the heat that was bothering him, he lost consciousness. He died in his wife's arms."

Meursault smelled of sweat and deodorant. It seemed he had just come up from the basement where he'd been running and lifting weights for the last two hours. That's how he spent his time. In the evening, he played a round of poker, routinely cheating, or indulged in a Russian card game with the Turgenev clan or even with Madame de Sévigné and Madame de Grignan. In the afternoon, he read spy thrillers or used the computer to keep his mind alert.

I had just risen quite late, as was my habit since arriving at the Annex two months earlier, and I was starting my day while Meursault's was already well underway … I hadn't heard the slightest sound during the night. My room at the end of the hall wasn't too far from the Turgenevs'. Despite always having been a light sleeper, I'd known nothing of what had happened right next to my bedroom, while Meursault, whose room was much further from the Turgenevs', had been awakened by the old Russian's moaning. Did the melatonin tablets that Celestino had bought for me contain something other than a sleep hormone? For more than a month, I'd been having trouble getting up and properly doing any sort of exercise … I'd lost the physique I'd maintained for two decades. A morning run on the treadmill in the basement seemed like a preposterous activity, and I quickly gave it up. Meursault, who was in great shape, had heard the Turgenevs' commotion. He had talked with Saturna to find out if protocol allowed us to see a doctor. Following his advice, she had immediately called Celestino, who was sleeping in another apartment building nearby, but before he could even determine whether or not he should alert the doctor, Turgenev had expired. The old lady was crying in the kitchen this morning. She was being consoled by Morel, the apartment's official mourner.

I had just heard all the facts reported by Meursault. He was going to attend to his own affairs. His access to the basement had been delayed because two women from the Organization had come to collect the body. They had talked about an autopsy, but Meursault didn't really think that would happen. He wanted to unnerve me, murmuring in his warm voice and Swiss-German accent, "Anna, my sister, Anna, don't you see anything coming? You actually believe this indigestion story … well, not me. I'm going to take a shower, meine Schwester, don't you want to come with me? They may have poisoned the old man. *Natürlich*." And with that, he disappeared.

I didn't linger but grabbed *Crime and Punishment* before heading to the kitchen to make myself a late breakfast. Clearly neither Saturna nor Celestino had gone shopping. The refrigerator was pitifully empty. The old Russian's death had interrupted the senseless daily routine that ruled the Annex and to which I'd grown accustomed since arriving almost two months earlier. I wondered where my companions were. They usually occupied the kitchen and talked among themselves, all while ignoring me. Not seeing them there giving me the cold shoulder was troubling. I picked up an old piece of bread lying on the counter and smeared it with the last bit of blueberry jam in the jar … I might have been poisoning myself too, but under the conditions of detention that still applied to me, like those that had been Anne Frank's, to refuse food was to slowly commit suicide. I had no choice but to trust my jailers and believe they wished me well. Nevertheless, I promised myself to keep an eye out, between the reading of two books. It was quite possible that the old Russian had died of natural causes. At dinner, he typically breathed like a seal and took medications for his heart and blood pressure that his own wife gave him at least three times a day. These facts were enough to reassure me. The intense heat wave of this interminable, blazing-hot summer was beginning to aggravate all of the Annex's occupants, even me—and I was 35 years younger than the deceased … Pittsburgh's climate, as Celestino laughingly told me, did not suit me at all …

I washed my jam and bread down with black tea and then went back to my room to read. My companions were all holed up in their own spaces behind closed doors. The Russian diplomat's death called for silence, an affectation of reverence. We would wait for midday and, more importantly, for some food before sharing our impressions. The loss of a member of the Annex, even one as ill-tempered and spiteful as Turgenev, was going to undermine our morale. Every community has a heightened desire to save its own. If we weren't careful, Turgenev's absence might, like a phantom limb, remind us of our living conditions, our confinement, and even our imminent extinction.

At the end of the winding hallway, I saw Dors Venabili, who was monitoring the comings and goings as she lingered outside the Turgenevs' room. I had to pass her to get back to my room, and as I drew near, I saw Mumu nestled in Morel's arms. The old lady had left the door open, hoping to receive the Hotel

Budapest's condolences. On the wingback chair, facing Madame Mumu, sat Madame de Sévigné. Her daughter remained standing further back, displaying a false look of regret. Sévigné and Grignan both felt how greatly their presence comforted the old lady ... This courtesy call increased their importance in their own eyes. They, who had worked hard to ignore the Turgenevs for weeks and who had made mincemeat of them at every card game they had finally deigned to play with them, now apologized for not having gotten to know the couple better. The death could only bring Madame Mumu and the two aristocratic kinswomen closer ... They made themselves a little community of women tested by life and by men. Sévigné could not keep herself from hinting to Mumu that Turgenev, whom she did not know, had perhaps shown his wife something other than love and gratitude. Mumu had never thought of things in such terms, but on second thought, yes, it was true: Turgenev hadn't been an angel, and look where he'd gotten her ... Now she was alone in a frightful prison, despite the support she felt.

Even as she recounted the sacrifices she'd had to make for her husband, she kept an eye on the hallway, undoubtedly hoping to receive other visits from the Annex's occupants. She was peeved when she caught sight of me. She gave me a look filled with anger. In the laughable performance of her bereavement, Mumu couldn't smile at me. To the contrary ... Her hatred of me was fortified by misfortune. It allowed her to redefine her place in the world order. My irritating presence reminded her that there were good people, like her, and despicable creatures, like me. So I went on my way without greeting her. I had no interest in making peace with the old woman or defending the woman I once was. Turgenev's death made no difference to me, one way or the other.

I started thinking about the long and famous novella, *The Death of Ivan Ilyich*, in which Tolstoy describes the death throes of a high-court judge. Throughout my life, I had often thought of Ilyich's end, especially at the time of my mother's death. The very artificial situation in which we found ourselves at the Annex and the connections that my companions were trying to stitch together among themselves by leading their life as if nothing was wrong reminded me of the Russian writer's tale. The story begins with Ilyich's burial during which neither his widow nor his daughter nor his work colleagues demonstrate true sorrow or great compassion toward the deceased. The judge has led a life built on the conventions and lies that society imposes. During his long illness, Ilyich discovers death, the one we conceal behind the monotonous daily grind, the one we forget as the hours tick by. In fact, it's through his descent toward a death he never imagined that Ilyich finally understands the vanity of his existence and that of the creatures surrounding him.

Although I saw the Annex as being a little society as phoney as Ilyich's bourgeois milieu in Russia at the end of the 19th century, I wondered if, at the time of his death, the Annex's old Mr. Turgenev had had any awareness of the foolishness of his family and of his own personal history. I doubted it … He had been caught off-guard and must have believed that he would still escape his own demise. He had neither the opportunity nor the desire to seize the marvelous yet terrible chance that death was offering him. It must be said that Ivan Ilyich Golovin had had a great deal of time to experience his death, not to mention the three days and three nights of suffering during which he'd howled in pain.

Presumably Turgenev had had no desire to become a Tolstoyan character, and that seemed a bit sad to me. In my line of work, I'd seen many people die, without ever observing in anyone any sort of preliminary visitation from death. On the contrary, there was always some kind of astounded surprise in the eyes of those I had killed, as if dying had never factored into their concept of life. As an Organization agent, this attitude had seemed normal, even if it contradicted many of the stories I'd read when I was younger as well as the last months of my mother's life. Despite the sadness, when her death was approaching, my mother and I had had little epiphanies. During my years of espionage when I knew that I was probably destined to die quickly at the hands of an assassin, I hadn't forgotten the intensity of the truth that mortality reveals. While avoiding my end, I awaited that last moment with curiosity. Perhaps that's how I'd become attached to Anne Frank who, despite her young age and her wish to live, had seemed able to sense her own vulnerability as well as that of all the others around her. Shut away in my own Annex, I couldn't help but worry a little about the absence of future Ivan Ilyichs or even of potential Anne Franks.

I thus spent the afternoon reading the short story about Ilyich, which I found on the little e-reader that Celestino had given me, loaded with ancient or recent texts that the Annex library couldn't have had. The events called for neither Dostoevsky nor Oksanen, but instead for Tolstoy. And it seemed to me that in spite of myself, I lingered over Celestino's suggestions because in the days following my arrival, he had advised me to search my readings for elements that would help me understand what I was facing. I could thus "shine a light on the future's dark matter," as he'd said, quoting an author I had to struggle to identify. That's why I knew that although the Annex had been instilled with a stern atmosphere that mimicked a meditation, we'd all be back around the dining table in the evening, as if nothing had happened. Tolstoy knew what vain and fearful people we are. Hadn't he written: "… this incident of a church service for Ivan Ilyich could not be a sufficient reason for infringing the order of the session—in other words, that it would certainly not prevent his unwrapping a new pack of cards and shuffling them that evening while a footman placed fresh candles on the table: in fact, that there was no reason for supposing that this incident would hinder their spending the evening agreeably."?

The Annex members would therefore continue to play cards after the meal that Saturna would prepare, using her superior skills to try to make us forget our petty concerns. They would laugh a little less and would lower their voices. They would be missing a playing partner, but very soon the joy would return, and one of us would replace the dead man. Gregor Samsa, the Hotel's other outcast, the one I was playing against, would take Turgenev's place.

That is why that afternoon, when I heard Celestino let out a scream and yell, "But my God, what has she done, what has she done?," I did not imagine for one second that Madame Turgenev had committed suicide by hanging herself from a chandelier suspended from the ceiling in the basement's great hall. I didn't even bother to leave my room. Moortje, also accustomed to our host's grotesque Commedia-dell'arte-worthy farces, lazily left her spot next to my pillow to come stretch out against my calves. Celestino was shouting himself quite hoarse, warning us not to come downstairs because he had just cut down Madame Mumu's body, but Moortje and I were certain that old lady Turgenev had not ended her life just hours after her husband's death. Neither the despair nor the imagined disgrace she had experienced since her confinement to the Annex had made her want to kill herself. Earlier, Madame de Sévigné had treated her with kindness; Morel had spent a long time comforting her; Meursault—the better to understand something about her husband's death, which he found highly unnatural—had certainly been attentive to her pain, gazing with his beautiful movie-spy eyes into hers; and lastly, Gregor Samsa had doubtless told her that, while he knew life's wounds, he could not imagine the torment that she, Madame Mumu, was suffering. I knew that this parade of the Annex's occupants through her room must have reassured old Madame Turgenev. She had clearly seen the symbolic capital conferred by the death of her spouse. It would allow her to live well for a year or two, pitied by all her fellow detainees. If the old lady had strung herself up, it wasn't because she was as tormented as Anna Karenina, nor was it because she had decided to follow the old Hindu rite of immolating herself on her husband's funeral pyre. No, Madame Mumu owed absolutely nothing to a Tolstoy, nor to an Indian lady novelist … She had acted like a Turgenev character until the end. I had no doubt about it. In any case, my presence in the Annex, however disagreeable it was for her, would have been reason enough to give purpose to her dreary existence. Hadn't she dedicated her life to the abhorrence of creatures like me … And lo and behold, thanks to little old me and my great insolence, she'd found herself in a very familiar frame of mind. She wouldn't have given up her role as inconsolable widow for anything in the world.

So as I lay on my bed, I put off finishing my reading of Tolstoy to think a little. Just two or three weeks earlier, Celestino had made me read *The God of Small Things*, the book by Indian author Arundhati Roy. In my room, he and I had lost ourselves for an hour or two in a discussion of the novel, and as one thing led to another, we had spoken about, among other things, the loathsome practice of sati, which obliges a widow to commit suicide upon the death of her husband. Celestino had chuckled at my indignation and incredulity, affirming that he himself had almost taken his own life 15 years earlier upon the death of his husband, an elegant, generous man whom he had loved passionately. I was an idiot for failing to understand the desperation that is love. It had nothing to do with feminism. According to Celestino, my years spent within the Organization had left me dimwitted. I couldn't see the passion in this ritual that I'd learned reading Gayatri Spivak when I was young. But that wasn't the point …

Celestino poked fun at the postcolonial reading I'd done as a good young leftist. He hoped that Arundhati hadn't awakened these outdated ideas in me and, if that was the case, I must have missed the book's greatest strength ... Somehow the conversation then took a different turn, and we went on to consider *Romeo and Juliet*, *Phaedrus*, and *Wuthering Heights* ... Celestino tried to show me that relationships are still much more complex than those that a little goose like me could imagine. So I thought again of Manuel Puig's book, *Kiss of the Spider Woman*, which was beginning to dominate my understanding of my connections to my jailer. Despite the clarity of the situation, were Celestino and I living out a narrative similar to the one that Valentin and Molina experienced in the novel? But Celestino was already speaking to me of Anna Arcadyevna Karenina about whom I had much to say. And I forgot the suicide of Indian widows and the murky relationship between Puig's two protagonists.

Had Celestino given me the Roy book in August so that we would discuss sati and so that I would accept without suspicion Mumu's suicide upon her husband's death? Was he that Machiavellian? Did he believe I was so easy to manipulate? Had the Organization planned everything? Which side was my host on? Was there something self-serving in his literary recommendations? Was he spending time with me, all the better to betray me? Why not? I had gotten very close to the Fosters for the sole purpose of infiltrating the enemy, and I had loved them, all the better to kill them. How much time did I have left to live? Were we all going to disappear, one after the other, the way they do in Agatha Christie's *And Then There Were None*, which Celestino had not suggested that I reread, but about which I was suddenly thinking? Was Meursault really my ally in the Annex, he who seemed to trust no one? What interest might this captive spy have in warning me of the danger? Had I really known him as a child? For two months, he had ceaselessly provided details about my childhood, which were disconcertingly accurate. So many questions crowded my brain, and I could not find their answers.

Nevertheless, despite the mental chaos I was feeling, it was quite clear to me, and to Moortje as well, that Mumu would never have made an attempt on her own life. Someone had killed her, and if we could not, as Celestino himself came to tell me, go down to the basement before two Organization representatives came to collect the second body of the day, it was simply because they hoped to keep us away from the scene of the murder. It was ridiculous to shield spies from corpses … While Celestino was making a tour of the rooms to tell each Annex resident about Mumu's suicide and the temporary closing of the basement, Morel was in the living room being consoled by Madame de Sévigné as he shed hot tears for his friend Mumu. I didn't need to leave my room and the softness of Moortje's fur against my warm legs to reconstruct the scene unfolding in a distant part of the apartment. The gigolo was having a nervous breakdown. Sobbing, he claimed he was guilty. He had left the widow alone just long enough for a short nap. How angry he was with himself! He hadn't seen anything coming even though, in such circumstances, he should have expected the worst. While Morel lost himself in prolonged lamentations, Gregor Samsa looked both appalled and nervous. He, the nuclear physicist, wasn't so foolish that he failed to harbour a great many doubts about Celestino. He most certainly wondered what was going to happen next. But he said nothing. Venabili, who had recognized that the situation was more complicated than Celestino was leading us to believe, also remained quiet. With Gaddafi, she had learned discretion. The years spent with the tyrant had taught her a certain number of lessons that could not be forgotten.

Were we all going to die? I quickly understood that no, death would not come for every one of us. Agathos could have easily eliminated us by sending a special commando unit to take us all out. They could simply tell anyone in the Organization who might have gotten wind of the story that the enemy had found us. No, a few of us were meant to testify that in Celestino's Annex, everything went without a hitch and, aside from a romantic tragedy (as the Turgenevs' assassinations would henceforth be called) and a few other minor matters, all of which would become hugely significant in the future, the Hotel Budapest operation would seem like a huge success. Appearances must be preserved because a few members of our community would survive this prison. How many of us? Who? I didn't know … I wasn't certain that I would number among those left alive, but I was betting that Morel would be the next on the list to die. I pictured him two or three months hence, riddled with bullets in the living room, shot in legitimate self-defence by Dors Venabili as he was preparing to kill Madame de Sévigné … You couldn't blame Venabili for defending the woman she'd been protecting 24 hours a day. Morel was playing for all of us the quintessential traitor in the farcical drama we'd been re-enacting at the Annex. His death would surprise no one. I was thinking of Morel's murder and seeing myself spared. I was behaving, I quickly realized, like the bourgeoisie in the Tolstoy short story that I had just reread. Like those whose curiosity led them to inquire about the details relating to Ivan Ilyich's end, I saw death as an accident specific to the Turgenevs or to Tolstoy's character, and that it would in no way affect me personally.

Moortje was snuggling up next to me; the day, though far too hot, was still beautiful. I had closed the curtains in my room to keep the sun out, and a makeshift fan cooled my body and the cat's a bit. Life was good. Simply put, I was free of the Turgenevs. I should thank Celestino, Morel, Meursault, or perhaps even the good Lord for having disposed of them. It seemed to me that my life in the Annex would be easier now.

Dinner that night bolstered my optimism. Celestino had removed the large table in the dining room around which the Turgenevs' ghosts might have come to haunt us. He had set up three small round tables. The one at the entrance was for Mata Hari, Morel, and Celestino, who joined the Annex's evening meal for a second time. The first had been at the supper held the day after my arrival. Since then, Celestino had decided not to eat with all the guests as a group. He preferred to manipulate us one at a time. I was at Meursault and Saturna's table. I very much liked the discreet woman who never talked about anything and with whom I didn't have to lie because we never exchanged a single word.

Madame de Grignan, Dors Venabili, and Gregor Samsa were seated at the third table. The food was already laid out on impeccable white tablecloths, so that Saturna didn't have to get up to serve us. That evening, we were meant to feel a very strong sense of belonging to our community. We ate like kings, first in silence, but the food and the alcohol soon caught us in the midst of great conversations. I understood that we would have a few weeks of feasting, something to make us forget the peculiar disappearance of our Annex companions … The food, which Celestino had planned for us, was to act like the keg in *The Little Cask*, Guy de Maupassant's splendid short story. It would function much as did the alcohol that Mr. Chicot gave to Mother Magloire. It would habituate us to indolence and contentment. It would intoxicate us with the pleasure of our meals, and soon, we would be domesticated. In Puig's novel, Molina had used roasted chickens to succeed in hoodwinking Valentin. He had asked the authorities who employed him for foods of all sorts, not just to fool his cellmate but also to bring him a little joy. Molina was eager to restore Valentin's health even as he helped poison his fellow inmate in the cell they shared. Thus Celestino could, while still intending to make us obedient and submissive, hope that we would have some very good times in his Annex. Indeed, I did not doubt Celestino's benevolence. But neither did I doubt his cruelty. Humans are capable of both the best and the worst, and when the two become entangled, something tremendously exhilarating thrills the deviants that we are.

I called upon this perversity within myself when, on the very night of the Turgenevs' deaths, I agreed to play cards with all of the Annex's other residents.

I was still capable of anything.

Chapter 9

"Wake up, Anna," Anne Frank whispered to me in a soft, childlike voice. "Wake up, little Anna. Don't let them get you. You mustn't. Don't surrender to death, please. I too knew moments of discouragement, you know, but you must not give in to despair. Your time will not come here. Wake up. You have to wake up. Make sure that you die somewhere else. In the open air. Definitely not in the Annex, it's me telling you this. We end up growing weak, here, dulled by the lack of space … One day, they came to get us. All eight of us! They'd decided to separate us, to tear us away from each other and take us very far away. During those years in hiding, I'd been so afraid this would happen, that I'd no longer be allowed to live with Papa, Mama … And all of a sudden, there they were, searching everywhere. They ransacked our cupboards, destroyed our lives with their boots. They made a hellish noise in the place where for more than two years we'd spoken in whispers, where we'd acted as if we no longer existed … We had believed that no one thought about us any more … But what can I say, they had nothing else on their mind … And yet, it was a relief … This is how I saw the Dutch sky again, Anna! One day I was newly dazzled by the sun outside, and on another day, the gentle rain caressed my cheek. But you know how the story ends. I … Wake up already!"

Anne Frank was there, sitting on my bed, right next to my suffering body. To better watch over me, she had perched on a pure white cushion with Moortje on her knees. The cat seemed quite happy to have his mistress back after so many years, and he purred with contentment! He smiled like the Cheshire Cat. With her slender, ink-stained fingers, Anne Frank caressed my hair, deftly arranging it on my forehead. A starched little black dress, hiding her undernourished body, leaned toward me. But her beautiful unscathed face—her eternal face, the one seen in the photos from that era—studied me with a kindness that I'd rarely experienced in my life. The rebellious curls of her mane were held back by a little gold barrette on the right side of her head, and her white Peter Pan collar brought an unexpected light to her dark silhouette. Anne Frank had returned to persuade me to live. With great tenderness, she begged me not to pass away during the night. She reminded me of the trips I'd made to Amsterdam so that I could visit her on Prinsengracht. It was there, close to her, that I had known true moments of consolation.

I had discovered the Annex when I was seven, in the company of our German teacher and the girls who boarded at Berg. Enchanted by this place where, even back then, I'd already felt at home, I had returned with great frequency. And I returned very recently … Did she remember having met me? Had she pretended to perish way over there, when in fact she'd settled permanently in the Annex, right in the middle of her flamboyant adolescence, one too grandiose for the times? How had she remained the magnificent young girl I felt beside me? Had she been hiding all this time? I was trying to form sentences so I could chat with Anne. I'd often imagined that I was talking with her, and questions tumbled about in my frenzied mind. But the words quickly became a formless mash in my mouth; they clumped together to form a soft dough with no specific shape. They came out of me in a muffled and somewhat hoarse groan without ever having found any density. It was a retching of words.

I was making a massive effort to shake myself out of it, but as soon as my mind attempted to put a few ideas together, it fell back into a black hole filled with even bleaker nightmares that overlapped to create bizarre shapes. I had wanted so badly to talk with Anne Frank, but I couldn't manage it. Horrible, distorted images from different pasts jostled each other inside my aching skull. The head of Gregor Samsa—who died in despair, having ingested bleach, just two weeks after the Turgenevs—seemed to be emerging from the chest of drawers in my room, while my friends the Fosters, killed by my Glock before my arrival at the Annex, lay motionless in an immense birthday cake right beside my bed. And then finally, in a big mass grave near the bathroom, the agents I'd eliminated during my twenty years of loyal service to the Organization were piled up, one on top of the other.

I remembered that a few hours earlier, I had swallowed, with a little rice water and according to his precise instructions, the medications that Celestino put in my mouth. He gave me Seconal tablets, which would help me endure the pain. That's what he'd ordered. He couldn't call the doctor: After all, we couldn't risk putting the Annex's inhabitants in danger for every little scratch ... But in his opinion, I was suffering from nothing more than an extremely bad case of indigestion that would pass more quickly if I could just calm down. The Seconal would do the trick. It seemed appropriate. My, but I had a gift for exaggerating everything! What a wimp I was proving to be! A relaxant was just the thing!

Seconal had been withdrawn from the barbiturate market at the beginning of the 2000s. I knew that perfectly well, and despite my terrible weakness, I wondered how Celestino had managed to obtain the powerful sleeping pill. In 1970, Jimi Hendrix had died of an overdose of Vesparax, which is largely made up of Secobarbital. Did my jailer want to make sure that I died like a rock star, from the abuse of prescription drugs? He'd probably found a way to read my mind because he'd told me while putting a red tablet in my hand that he'd procured the precious little pills in Russia. A fortune on the black market! They still manufacture them over there, and he knew how to find them: It was the only thing that managed to give him a few good hours of sleep! Even though he worked like a dog during the day to exhaust himself! With the safe houses, it never stopped! What a job! If he'd only known … But the night had never been his friend. Nothing to be done about it. The benzodiazepines that had flooded the market had a reputation they didn't deserve. It was like everything else in this world … Nowadays, they got rid of anything that remained effective.

Despite the suffering that kept me from thinking, I had laughed to myself over Celestino's pompous speech. I found the situation grotesque, ridiculous. "The Russians were and still are big poisoners," I had reminded him with difficulty. From the time of Potemkin up until the most recent cases … As Celestino knew, I had even worked on a case involving Novitchok. The Russians could not serve as a reference for an Organization agent like me. This was not a recommendation! And besides, when I was very young, I'd read Jacqueline Susann's *Valley of the Dolls*, a global best-seller at the time. My drug-addled mind seemed to be reliving scenes from the book. Instinctively, I did not want the last fictional character that I found myself embodying to resemble one of the women from that novel. If I survived my "extremely bad case of indigestion," I had no desire to be craving my little dolls, my scarlet-coloured pills. Upon hearing my confused, disjointed words, Celestino had cracked a smile. I had recognized a pain in him that was communicated by a small, sad grimace. But he had rapidly resumed his everyday expression to tell me with feigned lightheartedness, "Bella, you have no choice, you must trust me, whether I'm the good Lord or the Devil incarnate. The Russians are our enemies, of course, but that doesn't stop us from acknowledging their talent, for heaven's sake! *Madre de dios!* We shouldn't just belittle our adversaries. We must know their strengths. What's more, the safe houses of this world are full of people like you who didn't believe strongly enough in the Russians' power, and now here you are, in quite a bind ... Touché, no? Good, good, good ... Lie down, my dear, I'll take care of you. Your room ... What a state you've left it in! It's not very nice to look at ... And Saturna tells me that she'd already cleaned it! With mop and sponge ... I don't believe her for one second or else she's totally useless, that one! But more importantly, you're feeling poorly. You are truly dirty, dirty, dirty ... I must wash you. It's just that you're still a diva—yes, you—even when you're suffering! You, the queen of the hideout, you're like me, you need servants ... I am your lackey, after all. Russian or not ... At your service, your majesty ..."

I was in torment. The acute pain had begun the previous evening when, immediately after the meal, I'd gotten an excruciating stomach-ache. I'd endured vomiting and diarrhea, both unrelenting in their efforts to empty my guts within a few hours. Then I'd developed horrible cramps, followed by intermittent blackouts during the night and again in the morning. Clearly dehydrated, I'd fallen into a sort of comatose slumber. Because I hadn't appeared at either breakfast or lunch the next day, Saturna had come to check on me. It was Sunday, and on Sundays, Celestino did not stop by the Annex. Saturna had found me amidst my own effluvium, covered in various foul-smelling fluids that I'd allowed to drain out of me since I no longer had the strength to get up. I'd even driven away Moortje, whose return and presence I'd awaited in the middle of the night. In vain.

Upon seeing my alarming condition, Saturna had immediately alerted Celestino. She'd started scrubbing the room clean, not knowing where to begin. She couldn't take care of me. The boss had forbidden her to do so. Since Turgenev's death, the health of the Annex members was no longer her responsibility. Not under any circumstances. The cleaning, on the other hand, she was allowed to handle. Poisoning might also be among her tasks. So I told myself when I felt her touch my forehead, which she declared to be burning hot. I thought of the meals that she prepared so well … The night before, I'd feasted on an Indian dish of very spicy spinach whose aroma had filled the Annex all afternoon. She must have added something to my extremely appetizing food to make me die in excruciating pain. Who was this woman?

During the past months, I had taken little interest in her. I'd welcomed her presence like that of a loyal servant, an ally, an outstanding cook who could want only the best for me. Maybe I'd been fooled by her name, Saturna, which reminded me of Tristana's kind housemaid in the story by Pérez Galdós. Had Celestino given her that nickname so that I wouldn't be suspicious of her? Was Saturna in league with our jailer? Did she know what had caused the deaths of the two Turgenevs at the beginning of our incarceration? Did she know the truth about the recent disappearance of Morel, who had headed for the hills, hoping to escape organizations from here and elsewhere and return to a pre-espionage life? What had become of Morel? He couldn't have gone very far. I had foolishly hoped he'd been able to get away. Was Saturna still a household servant or, rather, did her role as a vaguely sexy maid enable her to kill members of the Annex with total impunity and without arousing the least suspicion?

Called by his Saturna, Celestino had arrived very quickly; at least that's what I'd thought when I saw him enter my room. I had welcomed him as both my savior and my executioner. I was pleased that Celestino would be the one accompanying me to my death, since he bore the greatest responsibility for my elimination. I had thought from the beginning that Celestino was trying to poison me. He was looking for a way to murder me. He was the one—the only one, after all—who wanted to harm me … That's what I kept telling myself … Saturna wasn't to blame. For some time now, I'd been playing the role of Valentin Arregui, whose betrayal pervades *Kiss of the Spider Woman*. Celestino made a fairly credible Molina. But to my eyes, Judas was preferable to Meursault. At least Celestino would talk to me about literature until the end. He'd be able to give me that old soft-soap to help me endure my dying moments.

I'd been in the Annex for six months, and my relationship with Celestino had evolved. He and I spent afternoons drinking very smoky Russian tea in my room. He said he bought the "Caravan from the Orient" from a Chinese couple at a little boutique in Pittsburgh. We alluded to Anne-Marie Schwarzenbach's works and even Yasushi Inoué's books, lingering over the one where the author describes how Mr. Rikyu, the Tea Master, kills himself by committing hara-kiri. We discussed the need for suicide, not from the practical point of view that we understood as secret agents, but with an approach that we hoped was more philosophical. On Sundays, the only day when Celestino left me in the lurch to go visit, he told me untruthfully, an old aunt who lived in one of the city's seedier neighbourhoods, I missed him terribly. We spoke about books, which I enjoyed. Between the two of us, we had formed a formidable book club whose sole idea had, however, deeply disgusted me when it had been mentioned during the welcome party. Neither Celestino nor I ever discussed our past lives, unless it was to share ready-made or made-up anecdotes and stories about the hotel in Cuba, imaginary lovers, or the circumstances pertaining to the discovery of a certain female author. Celestino created fictions for me with his life or with someone else's, and I largely kept quiet about my past, which I'd lost interest in a very long time ago. Nevertheless, I did, through our exchanges about literature, say disturbing, curious things about myself without appearing to do so. At least that's the lie that kept me going. Every day, I eagerly awaited Celestino. I needed to hear him and talk to him. I was, as he told me with a burst of laughter, his beloved patient, his Marie Cardinal … The perfect Socrates, he tried to make me give birth to words. And even though he clearly detested *The Words to Say It*, "that old-fashioned book, with its nauseating feminism," he pretended to understand that I could adore that kind of book, which suited the women of my time … I could not comprehend what drove me toward this wretched man. How could I have accepted the development of such a bizarre relationship? My stay in the Annex had totally changed me. I no longer recognized myself. Where did this passivity come from? Had I simply rediscovered my love of literature? Had I been deceived by the Organization? By myself? I had murdered two people, the Fosters, to whom for two years, I'd become far too attached. Who was I? A monster? A boring civil servant? Was Saturna putting diazepam in my food? I didn't know how to interpret my lack of a fighting spirit, and I had ultimately given up trying to understand myself. Celestino, however, always guessed what I might be thinking, keeping up a strange and accurate dialogue with my silence. Lola and Moortje, who had truly adopted me, managed to get along well in my room every day between the hours of four and six. Except on Sundays … Untouched by time, far from the world, the animals watched over my almost daily encounters with Celestino. I didn't miss my freedom. It would have been missed by that very violent character whom I'd been able to play during my years with Agathos and whom I had still been when I'd arrived at the Annex. Since then, I've had time to read and, to be honest, I was in the Montreal apartment only for meals and for the time I spent in Celestino's company. The rest of the day, I spent my time in Beckomberga, Lahore, Moscow, London, Quebec, or Wisconsin with Anna Karenina, Jean-Le Maigre, Achilles, Jane Eyre, Ursule Mirouët, Lily Bart, Anna Estcourt, Erika Kohut, or G.H.

Over the past few months, Meursault had ended up saying very little to me. He had warned me: Celestino was working for the Russians. He was a double agent. At first, I hadn't taken Meursault's warnings seriously, and then, over time, I had begun to realize that he was probably quite right. Presumably, he had not lied to me when he revealed his mission to ensnare our host. And soon he would have something to prove that Celestino was betraying the Organization. But Meursault knew that his assassination in the basement could be covered up as "a freak accident on the treadmill that caused a sudden death." Nevertheless, he remained hopeful that he could expose Celestino's true identity … But as for me, what did I have to hope for in post-Annex times?

"I must scrub you clean … I'm hard at work, even on my day off … My old aunt from Pittsburgh's slums won't have her soup this week. She'll go into a jealous rage or die of hunger. I'll tell her I was helping a younger woman, perhaps that will cheer her up."

Celestino gave me a second dose of Seconal without the least bit of resistance from me: I was having terrible stabbing pains in the pit of my stomach and lower down as well, in my intestines. I was ready to take whatever the head of the Annex was gently stuffing down my throat.

He urged me to take a shower, while he would wash the sheets and the mattress cover that he had put on the bed a few days earlier, just in case … I'd been suspicious of this meddling with my bed, but in this instance, I'd decided that I couldn't pick a fight with my jailer, and I preferred not to think that he could be hatching a plot. Seeing that I was too ill to get up and go to the bathroom, he decided to clean me up.

"I spent a long time as a nurse for the elderly … In another life. As people get older, they become slovenly. I killed them one by one, my old ladies, I liberated them from life. But that's another story. You've read Hervé Guibert? Yet another homo that I enjoy

… In *Cytomegalovirus*, his hospitalization diary, he writes about nurses in Tübingen who were killing their patients. That was me, those German nurses. I speak *Hochdeutsch*. You remember those women, your two guard dogs? They took me for an Otto. But I still learned to take excellent care of my patients … I find it useful here … What a time that was, the 1980s to the 1990s! AIDS … People were dropping like flies. I took care of so many friends … I guided them toward death … It had to be done. I am a man of duty … So you don't have to worry, I know how things are done, and now, right away, I'll find you a pretty white shirt that I'll put on you after I've caressed your body with a sponge full of sweet-smelling soap. You can't get up, I can see that. I'll do it bit by bit, you won't get cold. First your throat and the back of your neck, your face, your mouth, your chest, and the small of your back. And so on. It will also help bring down your fever." And while he was talking to me, Celestino had gone off to find a big washcloth to clean me up. He also returned from the bathroom with a small basin that he'd found who knows where, probably under the sink, and in which he'd put a big bar of soap that smelled nicely of lavender.

"I'm going to have to wipe you off, my dear, I'm going to remove your panties, which are stained with your excrement, and then I'll wash you all over. Turn over a touch, so that I can scrub you clean. I see … You can't. Really, you aren't strong … Wait, good … I'm washing you. Just stay still, and please don't worry … Yes, like that … Like that and a little bit this way … carefully, turn a little more, like that. Perfect. Spread your legs a little, yes, like that. Fear not, we're almost done, there … there … good. The water's not too cold? Not too hot? I'm also going to wash your hair. Like this … There … Now I'll rinse … At least your pubic area is well-shaved, nothing can get stuck in the hair, you were a girl with foresight, though you wouldn't think so to look at you. Not like our Lola—I always have to decontaminate and inspect her so that she doesn't bring vermin into my bed. We've developed the habit of sleeping together. Where is she, my little one? Ah! In the bathtub, on the sheets … Well, isn't that just fine, she wants to be as dirty as you, our Miss Lola … I'll see to that later … Shoo, skedaddle, Lolita mia …"

I was uncomfortable being washed down in this way by this man—undoubtedly my executioner—but sick as I was, I had no choice but to accept the pampering I'd been given. I had languished in my pain and my waste throughout the night. The fact that Celestino could momentarily erase the traces of my illness brought me unexpected comfort. The washing of my body was like a purifying ritual. I felt that the ablutions had just cleansed me of an ancient sorrow.

My host had opened the window, drawn back the curtains. He had already called Saturna. She briefly helped him to move me first to one side of the bed, then to the other, while he put clean covers and linens back on the bed. I still had the feeling that someone was stabbing me in the gut, but there was nothing left inside my body that I might have expelled.

Celestino finished by spritzing me with a cologne whose scent reminded me of the perfume that he wore each day when he came to read to me. He was in the process of using my body to produce his own creation. I let myself be lathered up and doted on like a child. I must mention that the Seconal was working its magic. It paralyzed me with contentment.

I ended up falling asleep without even realizing that Celestino had made me put on a long white shirt, which I was wearing when I woke up.

"You were shouting in your sleep," Celestino said, whereupon he had me sit up and swallow three spoonfuls of rice water. "You were having bad dreams, you've been resting for three hours. You look a little better, despite everything. The nightshirt suits you beautifully. Tell me."

"I have a terrible headache, and my stomach feels as if it's being repeatedly attacked by an electric drill, but it's not as bad now," I murmured in a faint voice. "The nausea has gone a bit. I feel like the bloating is starting again lower down. Sleeping helped me. And then, I had—I think—a sort of epiphany."

"Hold on, take another Seconal, open wide, you ninny, otherwise you're going to choke, with or without an epiphany. That's not a better way to go, you know. Even if it might be quicker than your poisoning. You think that Meursault put something in your food? I don't trust that one. You never mention him to me any more. Are you sleeping with him? No, I doubt it … I'm more your type … You're just delicate, and Indian food doesn't agree with everyone … I once had something similar. I'm very careful about what I put into my mouth. You should do as I do … Don't think about the pain, don't get upset. This whole crisis is caused by anxiety. Let's talk a little about something else, it'll distract you."

Celestino knew as well as I did that this was not merely indigestion or a case of nerves. Someone—clearly Celestino and not Meursault—had tried to kill me or was in the process of finishing me off. The Seconal had given me sound advice. Through a few strange dreams, the scene where Celestino washes my body had come back to me. It appeared to me as some kind of very clear hallucination. While washing me, my reading partner had made me reenact a whole portion of *Kiss of the Spider Woman*. Molina knows that Valentin is being poisoned by the food because Molina's the one that betrayed him and who recommended this form of debilitation. Nevertheless, he lovingly cares for his "friend" when he is weak … Together Celestino and I had admirably reinterpreted this extraordinary scene between Puig's two protagonists. I had, somehow, played my role perfectly. The illness had prompted my words and my frailty …

I wasn't even angry. Puig had secretly kept me company since the beginning of my Annex life and, although I hadn't laid hands on the text again, I accepted the meaning that it brought to my new life and to my passing. Even though he was there to murder me, Celestino would help me transition from life to death. In a twisted way, he would take pity on me until the end. He would not save me. We could talk about life and death side by side, and these moments, as horrific as they might appear, already seemed precious to me. I had always imagined a swift end to my life. I was, however, was going to be tortured to death … Celestino was taking pleasure in tormenting me. He inflicted upon me my own desire to die with him by my side. I'll never know what he really wanted from me, but I—a secret agent who'd liquidated multiple people—was ready to beg him to stay with me. Soon, if the acute pain persisted, I would ask him to finish me off with my pistol. I didn't have the strength to reach my gun. I doubted that I'd regain any sort of energy. The poison and the Seconal were creeping through my body. I might also die of an overdose. That would be better. People would conclude that for several weeks, I had been asking Celestino for something to help me sleep and that I had amassed enough pills to kill myself. And then, one day, Celestino would get caught. But not right away.

I almost immediately fell back to sleep again, while my companion was telling me something, I no longer remember what. When I opened my eyes, he was reading in the armchair next to me. He had been watching over me.

"Look what I found in your bookcase! I have to find a way to pass the time. The room is sparkling clean, and you're sleeping like a baby. My work is done … It's a fabulous novel, Schnitzler's *Fräulein Else*. What a coincidence! You aren't familiar with it, are you? You would have mentioned it to me … To save her father's honour, the heroine, a young girl whose first name is Else, must borrow money from a rich art dealer named Dorsday, I'm telling you his name so that you'll follow me, okay? You don't seem to be doing much better, but let me finish my story, and then I'll take care of your body … It will amuse you, I promise. The merchant agrees to loan Else the money to cover her father's gambling debt but only if she'll appear nude before him. With difficulty, Else agrees to this blackmail. She feels humiliated, dirty … Stories about an innocent young thing … It has a modicum of interest, psychologically speaking. Good, you'll see what happens next … Dressed in a black coat, she goes to the hotel to meet Dorsday. Eventually, she drops the coat and then faints. Humiliated at having been seen this way (what an idiot, this girl, really …), she wants to kill herself with sleeping pills. I didn't check to see if it's Seconal, hold on … The story ends before telling us whether or not she dies from them. You see the parallels with us? Do you believe that she dies from the overdose? In my case, I didn't have to blackmail you so that I could see you completely naked, right? You let it happen this afternoon. Rightly so. I washed you. You needed me and some soap … I'd seen you practically naked the first time we met, but it wasn't as good as it was today, I'll admit … You do know, however, that I don't like girls, only boys. So I couldn't fully enjoy the view. Only a little. Listen, alone as I am, I could take a woman to bed. I don't often get a chance to be in love, and with you, well, I love you and you know it. But recently, there was Morel, with whom I spent some very intense, very pleasant moments. The swine wanted to get away from me. He said that I was behaving like a jealous lunatic. Why not Charlus? … They found him dead … and it wasn't a pretty sight. Tough to imagine. He was such a magnificent boy … The others killed him. He preferred death over me … That's the way it is … What a little prick! His name was Alexis Beaufort. It's not important, but now that he's dead, I think that we can give him back his name. My handsome Alexis … I must bring bad luck. I inspire the urge to flee. In a certain sense, I'm responsible for his death. Well, okay, not entirely after all. Didn't you think Alexis was adorable? It was the Turgenevs or Samsa, it wasn't me. Not even indirectly. You think I would lie to you? No, of course not! Life here isn't easy … People worry themselves to death, have a heart attack, hang themselves, swallow bleach, or even have a very, very bad case of indigestion. They take too much Seconal … That's life at the Annex, as you and Anne Frank would call it. Listen, my dear, I hate seeing you this way. I've left you your pistol, your Sig Sauer, on the nightstand. Right next to you. I put the bullets beside it. You can think about it. I'm sure that you'll get better, but you know … Pistols, they reassure secret agents, don't they? Gives them the impression that they have some power over their life … If you're in too much pain, you'll use it, won't you? I don't want you to suffer unnecessarily. Because your terrible, terrible case of indigestion can last even longer, and why go through that? You'll see, okay … It's better with the Seconal, right? I had a good idea, but one never knows, right? You're still a secret agent who might like to end her life with dignity. I don't know … we shall see."

From the depths of my agony, I found the strength to say, "You're so kind, my friend … You're good for me. Give me a cigarette, they're right there on the dresser. I'm going to smoke one. You don't like the smell, but just this once … yes, just a bit of tobacco, everything's so normal. Please light it for me. You're a sweetheart to hold it for me … Thank you, and now, come lie down with me, Celestino, lie against me in the bed … I'm cold, so cold … It's been a few months since a human has slept up against my body. I'm going to die, Celestino, I know. Don't deny me your presence. I'm going to take you up on your offer of the gun, if I'm strong enough, but now … I … I need you … yes, another puff … You can tell other stories like the one about Else. Wonderful stories. So I can fall asleep. I like them so much … All these months, you kept me alive with your tales. The thing I was most afraid of, can you imagine, was that they'd separate us and put me in a different Annex. Forever … Can you believe it? I'm not even afraid of death any more, thanks to you, to you and to literature. Come lie down, here, right here … I'm begging you, you can't refuse a dying woman."

And as Celestino complied and came to take me in his arms, I kept speaking to him softly. His partial admissions, his invitation to a suicide worthy of an Organization agent no longer had any effect on me. I was going to kill myself, but I wanted to continue talking to my executioner. He stayed there, glued to my side. My last cigarette had been smoked. My executioner warmed my feet. The heat of his abdomen against mine somewhat eased my pain. I felt good. We were so close … Others would have kissed each other. My own mouth, so very close to his, then whispered, "*Kiss of the Spider Woman*, Celestino, *El beso de la mujer araña*, as they call it where you come from, you know, my dear Cuban friend? The book by Puig, the Argentinian. Why him? Why did you decide that this was the book was for us? Is it your favourite? I need to know. Why this book? You have good taste, but why?" Without moving, Celestino looked me in the eye and said almost lovingly, "I always wondered if you would notice, my darling … or if you would have the courage to talk to me about it. You've been running out of courage, over the last little while … Isn't literature marvelous?" And he planted a little kiss on my forehead. Happy, I fell into a perfectly contented sleep.

It was during this slumber that Anne Frank came to visit me … "Wake up, Anna, wake up, don't let them get you … do not die in the Annex …" I finally woke up … I was still in the arms of my assassin, who had dozed off. Yet I had turned over. I had my rear end against his warm belly. I was now facing the door and my dresser. Lola was quietly sleeping at our feet. We were among the blessed. The gods' chosen ones. Suddenly, I saw Moortje; he had just come out of one of his secret hiding places and gave me a funny look, smiling at me like the Cheshire Cat. Was this the animal that I had mistaken in my dreams for Anne Frank? I would have had a hard time admitting it.

Without any premeditation, I got up, grabbed my 9 mm Sig Sauer P228 Parabellum and loaded it. I took aim at Celestino's single astonished eye. He had risen to a sitting position, not understanding what was happening to us. Lola, who was still asleep, barked only when the three bullets were fired …

Celestino was, after all, like all the other corpses I'd seen. Hideous to look at. Literature could no longer do anything more for him.

Epilogue

From my apartment on Merwedeplein, I can see the tiny bronze statue of Anne Frank. She is carrying a satchel under her left arm. In her right hand, she holds a small suitcase. She looks into the distance, as if she was not or was no longer of this world. Anne Frank looks toward the future that she will not have, toward the History that quickly destroyed her. She does not linger over the children who run before her or even over the houses that surround her. Yet upon seeing her lifting her heavy bags like that, I picture her as being energetic as she walked across the city of Amsterdam on the morning of July 6, 1942, wearing layers of clothes despite the heat. Before the Annex at 263 Prinsengracht, Anne resided on Merwedeplein in a cluster of buildings grouped around a spacious courtyard that formed a square where children back then shouted despite the rain, as children still do today.

A short film made on July 22, 1941, a year before their move to the Annex, shows one of the Franks' neighbours on Merwedeplein. The happy young woman descends the stairs on her wedding day. At the window of her apartment, curious little Annelies Frank leans out for a moment to get a better look at newlyweds' elegant attire. It's the only document where Anne can be seen moving. Before the time spent at 263 Prinsengracht, the time of the Annex, Anne Frank led the life of a little girl who was inquisitive, intelligent, and most importantly—alive. From my own apartment, as I watch the little ones playing on the grass where Anne herself must have played, I see the statue coming to life, the bags taking flight, and Anne running after a hoop or a ball. I even hear her squabbling with her older sister or with Hanneli Goslar. She laughs with Sanne Ledermann, threatens Jacqueline van

Maarsen, approaches Hello Silverberg, and avoids Eva Geringer, who lives just on the other side of the square. Anne often runs into Michael Vellemann, an extraordinary magician known by the name of Professor Ben Ali Libi. The little girls keep a close watch over the comings and goings of this great illusionist about whom the neighbourhood folk whisper all sorts of things both amusing and fantastical. Vellemann lives at 59 Merwedeplein, next to the Franks, who live at Number 57. Occasionally, Anne laughs as she bumps into the Jewish Hungarian writer Andreas Latzko, who moved to Amsterdam, onto Merwedeplein, in 1933, the same year as the Franks. She giggles when she greets Herbert Lewyson Nelson, son of the great cabaret musician from Berlin, in front of the Kousenkliniek Laddervast, where Else Löwenstein-Golberg repairs stockings for the women of the neighbourhood.

Anne plays on Merwedeplein from 1933 to 1942. She goes to buy paper at the corner, from a small shop on Rooseveltlaan. At the Blankevoort bookstore, her father buys her the famous notebook with its red-checked cover in which she writes her diary.

I often go to Boekhandel Jimmink, as the bookstore Anne frequented is now called. Yes, I recently moved near the apartment where Anne spent her childhood. After Celestino's death, things happened quickly. Against all expectations, I recovered from my poisoning. I wasn't actually accused of Celestino's murder. Meursault helped me. He had collected sufficient evidence against our jailer. Even if he never really was Hélène Samroy's brother, the guy was watching over me. I was relocated to a different safehouse, far from Madame de Sévigné and her daughter Grignan, who had themselves been killed in their hiding place, according to the official story. Is it true? Mata Hari and her daughter could have changed their names and faces. In that case, they could be living happily in some African country or in Paris. Grignan might even have started dancing again …

My Annex was indeed situated in Montreal. Celestino had lied to me. After his death, I was moved to one of the city's suburbs. I lived there with real spies, who were tight-lipped and athletic. It was better that way. I got back into shape, and I spent my time exercising. One morning, after almost four years in hiding and shortly before the American elections in 2016, they let me leave. Agathos needed specialists like me who spoke Russian, and by then, the death of the Fosters had been long forgotten. No one else wanted to eliminate me. Times had changed. I didn't even take the time to tour the city. I didn't want to revisit the street where my grandparents had lived long ago. And once free, I very quickly acquired a Glock 9 mm. Then I bought a plane ticket to Amsterdam.

I rented an apartment there, on Merwedeplein. I had gone back to Prinsengracht, but Anne wasn't there. In the house-museum, there was only the little girl in hiding, the girl who wrote so that she would have a friend, the girl who could neither see the sky nor play on the grass. Now I live where Anne lived. Not where she practically died of boredom, not where she lived in terror. I therefore live far from the Annex.

I also saw Moortje again, the cat that Anne had left behind on Merwedeplein in 1942. She had allegedly been taken in by neighbours that same year. They'd said she'd died, that sack of fleas. Her new owners had had to get rid of her. But she had simply scampered off. After finding and then losing my Moortje in Montreal, I wasn't surprised to come across him in Amsterdam as I walked through Anne's former neighbourhood. He followed me all the way home, the little darling!

The apartment where Anne lived with her family from 1933 to 1942 now houses writers—political refugees—who must hide themselves away in order to write. I watch over them from my current living room whenever I'm not on a mission in Moscow or Saint-Petersburg.

Anne was a writer, and as such, we pay tribute to her.

But I think of her differently when I see her run and laugh on the lawn, when her statue comes to life.

She remains for me the little girl who has a cat named Moortje. She knows nothing of the Annex, or of History, which will prove to be appalling, or of the world that will tremble again and again.

Anne Frank enjoys life.

The rest—all the rest—is literature.

Translator's Notes

Page 14
The quotation from Jean Jacques Rousseau's *D iscourse on Inequality* was translated by G. D. H. Cole. https://www.files.ethz.ch/isn/125494/5019_Rousseau_Discourse_on_the_Origin_of_Inequality.pdf

Pages 15, 16, 22, 75
The quotations excerpted from Anne Frank's diary and translated into English are taken from *Anne Frank The Diary of A Young Girl*, edited by Otto H. Frank and Mirjam Pressler, translated by Susan Massotty. https://archive.org/stream/AnneFrankTheDiaryOfAYoungGirl_201606/Anne-Frank-The-Diary-Of-A-Young-Girl_djvu.txt and http://www.rhetorik.ch/Aktuell/16/02_13/frank_diary.pdf

Page 75
In her diary, Anne Frank refers to her cat Moortje as being a female although the cat's gender has been questioned elsewhere. For the purposes of this translation, the Moortje in Montreal is a male, as the author refers to this animal in the masculine.

Page 84
François René Chateaubriand's quotation is excerpted from *Memoirs from Beyond the Grave*, translated by A. S. Kline. https://www.poetryintranslation.com/PITBR/Chateaubriand/ChateaubriandMemoirsBookXXXVI.php

Page 84

Charles Baudelaire's quotation is excerpted from "Cats", translated by William Aggeler. https://www.best-poems.net/charles_baudelaire/les_chats_cats.html NB There are several translations of this poem, but Aggeler's most closely follows the French.

Page 102

Melissa Müller actually wrote that Lena Hartog, who worked as a cleaner in the warehouse at Prinsengracht 263, was told by her husband (also a warehouse employee) about the Jews in hiding there and that she then shared this information. There is no definitive proof of this theory. David Barnouw and Gerrold van der Stroom, *Who betrayed Anne Frank?* Netherlands Institute for War Documentation (NIOD), 2003.

Page 113

The quotation from Fourier is taken from *Le Nouveau monde industriel.* Portions of it were translated into English by John S. Dwight and published in the journal, *The Harbinger* ("New Industrial World." Translated by John S. Dwight. [Serial: II, 99, 113, 129, 145, 161, 177, 289, 305, 329, 343, 406.; III, 34, 57, 87, 117, 133, 182, 217, 260, 280, 297, 314, 330, 390.] as cited at https://www.libertarian-labyrinth.org/utopian-and-scientific/bibliography-of-the-works-of-charles-fourier/), sometime in the 1800s. (John Sullivan Dwight b. 1813 d. 1893.) I have not found any publication of the English version of this specific text.

Page 113

The quotation is from Chapter 3 of F. Scott Fitzgerald's *The Great Gatsby*. https://www.academia.edu/12185413/The_great_Gatsby_chapter_3

Page 124

The quotation translated into English and excerpted from Leo Tolstoy's *The Death of Ivan Ilyich* is taken from University of Minnesota Libraries https://open.lib.umn.edu/ivanilich/chapter/full-text-english/

Page 127

Agatha Christie's novel was originally titled *Ten Little Niggers* when published in Britain in 1939. In 1940, the title was deemed too offensive, so it was published as *Ten Little Indians* outside the United States and as *And Then There Were None* in the U.S.

About the Author

A major figure in Quebec literature, Catherine Mavrikakis has published quite a number of outstanding novels since her first was published in 2000, among them the remarkably intense novels *Le Ciel de Bay City*, *Oscar de profundis*, and *La Ballade d'Ali Baba*. An essayist as well, she has won many awards and distinctions. She was a finalist for the Governor General's Award (French theatre category) in 2008 and won no less than three awards for *Le Ciel de Bay City*: the Grand prix du livre de Montréal, the Prix littéraire des collégiens, and the Prix des librairies du Québec. In October 2021, she was in Frankfurt as part of the official Canadian delegation for Canada's guest of honour program at Frankfurter Buchmesse. Her work has been translated into German and Italian, among other languages, and is also published in France by Sabine Wespieser Éditeur.

About the Translator

Kathryn Gabinet-Kroo was born and raised in Oregon and after earning a BA from Cornell University, she moved to Canada, where she has been a professional artist for over 45 years. While painting, teaching at a private art school, and raising a family, she earned her Master's in Translation Studies from Concordia University. Since then, she has been "working two jobs" from her studio in Montreal.

A freelance translator since 1996, she has worked for clients in the public and private sector including, among others, the Canada Council for the Arts, the Museum of Civilization, Fisheries and Oceans Canada, Environment Canada, and Éditions Québec Amérique. Her true passion is literary translation and since 2014, her French-to-English translations of six novels and two short story collections by Quebec authors have been published. A number of her translations of individual short stories and selected chapters have been published in literary journals, both on-line and in print.

Kathryn is a member of the Literary Translators Association of Canada (LTAC) and the Quebec Writers' Federation (QWF). In her downtime, she is a competitive ballroom dancer.

Printed by Imprimerie Gauvin
Gatineau, Québec